Danger! Bad Boy

Book Two of the

Beware of Bad Boy series

April Brookshire

ISBN-13: 9781499761443

April Brookshire

CHAPTER ONE

"Falling in love is like jumping off a really tall building.
Your brain tells you it is not a good idea,
But your heart tells you, you can fly."
-Anonymous

GIANNA

The whole way out of Colorado I'd expected red and blue flashing lights to come up behind us. Imagining Caleb and me being hauled into the nearest police station to wait for our parents to pick us up had not been fun. Driving down Interstate 70 into Utah, I'd let out a sigh of relief. My mom wouldn't think to look for us outside of Denver. Cece had texted me an hour ago asking what the heck was going on and why my mom had been blowing up her phone. My mom had even gone so far as to call Cece's mom.

Two seconds after texting her that Caleb and I had sort of ran away together, my phone started playing "The Jump Off" by Lil' Kim.

At Caleb's look, I asked, "What? Cece picked it."

"Figures," he muttered, shaking his head.

"What's up?" I asked breezily upon answering, as if I weren't on the run with my boyfriend.

"Gianna!" Cece screeched, making me pull the phone a few inches away from my ear. "Where the heck are you?"

"Somewhere in Utah," I told her. "Actually, we're coming up on a town called Richfield. It's late so we're checking into a hotel for the night."

"What the heck are you doing in freaking Utah?" Cece yelled into the phone.

"Promise not to tell anyone?" I asked, wanting to assure her secrecy and hopefully calm her down. "Especially my parents or yours?"

"Of course," Cece scoffed like it was a given.

Feeling scared, alive and crazy at the same time, I needed to confide in my best friend. "Caleb is taking me to Vegas!"

4

My phone beeped and I knew it'd be another text from my mom. She'd given up on calling a couple hours ago. Caleb had answered a call from his dad before we were even out of Denver. His dad wasn't happy about us taking off and was even less happy when Caleb informed him we'd be gone for a few days. At the same time, his dad was dealing with the emotional fallout of separating from his wife. Caleb had told him we'd be at a hotel for the next few days but he purposely failed to mention the hotel would be in Las Vegas.

"Aw!" Cece whined as I ignored my mom's text. "I want to go to Vegas!"

"Next time we'll go as a group," I assured her.

"Group road trip!" Cece squealed. I was sure the image in her head was like in commercials where friends on road trips had a crazy good time. The ones where the sun was shining, the windows were rolled down and nobody wore their seatbelt.

Caleb pulled off the freeway and into a gas station. At just past midnight in this small town there was only one other car in the lot, probably the clerk's.

"Look, Cece, I have to go, we're stopping at a gas station."

"Fine, but you better call me when you get to Vegas tomorrow!" she ordered, still sounding put out about not being invited.

"Of course," I replied on a yawn.

"Love you, Gigi!" she said. "Be careful!"

"Love you, too." I hung up the phone and got out to stretch my legs. Caleb was already pumping gas; filling up for the four hours we still had to drive tomorrow. "I'm going to get some snacks. Do you want something?"

Every once in awhile, at normal moments like this, it'd hit me how weird it was that we'd gotten together. How had this guy gone from being the bane of my existence to the center of my world in such a short period of time?

He looked as tired as I felt, but he hadn't complained once while driving over seven hours over the Rockies and through the Utah desert. "Gatorade, barbeque chips and cashews."

Having his order, I walked into the convenience store and headed straight for the bathroom first.

As I browsed the aisles, grabbing Caleb's snacks and a few things for myself, the middle-aged male clerk mostly ignored me while reading his car magazine. Actually, it was more like a car porno, with a girl in a bikini sprawled across the hood of a classic car on the front cover.

The bell on the door chimed and I looked up with a smile, expecting it to be Caleb. It wasn't. A shady looking guy in his early twenties headed straight to the back freezers where the alcohol was kept. Feeling suddenly nervous about being in a gas station in the middle of the night in the middle of nowhere, Utah, I snatched a bag of chips on my way up front to pay.

My arms were full and I clumsily dropped the items on the counter. "Can I get these in a bag, please?"

"Sure," the clerk answered, warily eyeing the skuzzy-looking shopper still lingering in the back.

Just as my purchase was totaled, the bell chimed again and Caleb strode in. I'd almost used my debit card then rethought it when I remembered that people were always tracked in movies that way. Instead, I handed the guy a twenty. Caleb grabbed the bag while I was given my change and ushered me out of the store.

He'd moved the car and was parked right outside the door. "Did you see that guy?" I asked him.

"Yep, that's why I came in to get you."

"Do you think he's going to rob the place?"

Caleb chuckled. "It'd be pretty stupid of him. He walked here, so it wouldn't take much for the cops to chase him down. He's probably just shoplifting."

"Oh," I said dumbly, wondering if we should call the police. Caleb didn't seem too concerned and the clerk had been eagle-eyed, so I figured the guy had it covered.

I still couldn't believe I'd taken off with Caleb like that. I intended on going back home when things had cooled off some. After having a little fun with my hot boyfriend in Vegas, of course.

Holy crap, my mom was probably going berserk right now. Maybe this wasn't such a good idea. I glanced over a Caleb as we pulled out of the gas station parking lot. "You do realize my mom is freaking out?"

His smile said he wasn't sorry. "She was doing that already. We just gave her something to really freak out about."

"Yeah, I suppose, but now she's going to spaz out even more. I'm so dead when we get back to Denver." Gripping my head in my hands, I added, "Not to mention the days of school we're ditching."

"I think this is a great idea. We needed to show your mom that we won't bow down to her bullying. I bet she's already regretting kicking my dad out."

"That was pretty bad," I commented, inwardly cringing at the memory. "You know, if they get divorced, we won't be stepsiblings anymore."

"A silver lining," Caleb muttered.

"So you'll still want to be with me if it's no longer taboo?" I teased him.

Coming to a stop in the parking lot of an economy hotel, he scanned my body up and down with unmistakable heat. "Still very interested."

"You better say that," I scolded with a fake glare.

Unbuckling his seatbelt, Caleb pulled out his wallet, sliding out his fake ID. "You stay here while I get us a room, princess. With no makeup you look younger and we don't need anyone asking questions." Before shutting his door, he ducked down to look at me. "Keep the doors locked."

He was gone for fifteen minutes and I was about to call his phone when I spotted him coming out. "What took so long?"

All I got was a sideways glance as he started the car. Finally, he said, "The nighttime front desk girl offered to join me in my room when her shift ended."

"What?" I asked in shocked outrage. Caleb was moving the car around the building to park in back. It kind of made me feel like he was hiding me. "Did you flirt with her?"

His smirk was answer enough. "Maybe a little. Got us a great discount on the room."

"I'm thinking I may just sleep in the car," I grumbled.

"She wasn't as pretty as you," he said cajolingly.

My scowl told him that wasn't going to get him off the hook.

His laugh irritated me even more. "I found her repulsive," he tried again.

"Liar," I accused, holding back laughter at how manipulative he could be. First he used his charm on that girl to get a cheaper room and now he was using it on me to get out of trouble for flirting with her.

Too bad for him I knew him so well.

Caleb handed me a keycard and grabbed our bags out of the trunk. I walked ahead of him to scan my keycard and hold the back door of the hotel open for him. "Room 206," he informed me while hitting the button for the elevator.

"So, what did you tell her?" I asked, still annoyed with him.

Caleb stood on the other side of the elevator staring at me, while biting his lip to stop from smiling. "Princess, I was just messing with you. The front desk clerk was an old dude who took forever checking me in because he was half-blind."

My mouth dropped open in a mixture of anger and admiration. "You suck, Caleb."

His shoulders were shaking in laughter as he ushered me out of the elevator ahead of him.

Quietly, in respect for the people sleeping in the rooms we passed, we made our way down the brightly lit hallway to our room.

Mad and at the same time relieved that my boyfriend hadn't been flirting with some hotel skank, I opened up my suitcase, digging through it for some pajamas and not finding any. "You forgot to pack me some pajamas."

He gave me a naughty grin. "Did I? Maybe you won't need any."

Going over to where he stood at the foot of the bed, I pressed my body against his. "Are we gonna *do it*?" I asked in a scandalized tone.

His eyes were hooded as he licked his bottom lip. His body was stiff as he gazed down. Relaxing visibly, he teased, "I'm offended, Gianna. You make me feel cheap. Don't you want to make love to me?"

"I don't remember love ever being mentioned between us," I said casually, feeling mixed up inside. Caleb didn't say anything in response, so to spare his player sensibilities and myself unneeded embarrassment, I went back to the original topic. "So, do you?"

He looked confused as he slowly asked, "Do I?" He must've still been on the second topic that I now desperately wanted to avoid. "Oh, um, I don't think that's a good idea," he said carefully. "I'm exhausted from the drive and I don't think you want your first time to be in some crappy hotel, in some crappy town in Utah. Especially not after the drama with your mom today. Plus, it should be special for you and I wouldn't want to put in a poor performance after driving all day."

Wow, if I didn't know better, I'd have thought Caleb was nervous at the prospect of having sex with me. His rambling was uncharacteristic. Was Mr. Sexy Player nervous about having sex with little ole virgin me? Interesting. And perhaps my chance at payback for his trick earlier.

"Caleb?" I said his name sweetly.

"Yes, Gianna?" Caleb's face wore a strange expression, a mixture of excitement and wariness.

"You wouldn't happen to be nervous at the thought of us having sex, would you?"

He hesitated before answering. "Maybe a little." His forehead wrinkled as he cleared his throat. "It's just that you're a virgin and I normally avoid sex with virgins, too much potential for disaster." He visibly shuddered. "On top of that, you're special to me. I don't want to fuck it up."

"Potential for disaster," I echoed his words. *Well that's a turn on*, I thought sarcastically.

Caleb seemed to recognize his poor choice of words in describing my state of virginity. He tried to recover by saying, "Not that I think it'd be a disaster between you and me. I just think if we are going to *do it* on this trip, as you so eloquently put it, then we should wait until we're in Vegas. When we aren't tired and we're in a nicer hotel."

"This is such a surreal moment. After all the guys who have tried to get in my pants . . . and I'm getting shot down." I shook my head in disbelief. "Amazing."

Caleb's lips turned up in a cocky grin. "I *am* enjoying the experience of you begging for it."

I shoved his chest. "I so wasn't begging."

"Whatever you say," he taunted.

I stroked his arm, giving him a flirtatious look. "We'll see who does the begging before this trip is over."

Moving away from him, I rummaged through his bag and pulled out one of his t-shirts. With my back still to him, I took off my clothes and stood in just my bra and panties. The bra went next. The chorus of that old R&B song by Tweet about stripping off her clothes began running through my head. The sound of him hissing in a breath made me smile. I had to bite my lip to keep from laughing as I pulled the t-shirt over my head.

Turning around to meet his dark eyes, I asked in the most innocent tone I could muster, "What?"

Standing up with clenched fists, his hazel eyes darker than usual, he rasped out, "I'm going to take a shower."

Right before he closed the bathroom door, I called out, "A cold shower?" The door slammed shut and a moment later the water turned on. I dropped onto the bed and gave my laughter free reign.

CALEB

Wrapping a towel around my waist before leaving the bathroom, I found Gianna already asleep on the bed, looking all sweet and sexy in my shirt. I couldn't believe she'd stripped in front of me. Even getting only the back view of her, it was the hottest thing I'd ever been privileged to witness. Amazingly, it was even hotter than two chicks making out.

How much hotter was the front view going to be? Not to mention the sex. Dammit, if I didn't stop thinking about it, I was going to need another shower. I pulled on some basketball shorts and slipped under the covers with her. Lying on my stomach, with one arm draped over her, I thought how nice it'd be to sleep with her like this all the time.

Especially after sex.

*****

The next morning, I came awake with my arms and legs wrapped around Gianna. Not able to resist her sleeping face, I woke her up by showering kisses all over it. She grumbled moodily and pushed my face away. "Go away, Caleb."

"It's Vegas time. Get your cute little ass up! We still have a few hours to drive and I'm hungry." I slapped her ass to get her moving.

She sat up while rubbing her eyes. "Fine, but I still have to take a shower before we leave." I was treated to a peek of her black panties as she slid off the bed. She might be right about me being the one to beg.

I got dressed while she was in the shower and looked around the room to make sure we didn't leave anything behind. Once she was dressed, I was more than ready to go. We went through a fast food drive-thru for breakfast and were finally on the road by midmorning.

Gianna turned her phone back on to listen to her messages. From the look on her face, I could guess that her mom's messages weren't offerings of a truce.

We couldn't stay away forever, so I decided to call my dad, to feel things out for when we did come home. He answered on the first ring, making me feel guilty if he'd been worried. The combination of separating from your wife and your son making off with your stepdaughter couldn't be pleasant.

"Caleb, where in the hell are you?"

"School?" I joked badly.

"Not funny. Is Gianna still with you?"

"Yep."

"You need to take her home to her mother. Julie is irate."

And obviously taking it out on my dad. "No shit. She was *irate* before we left."

"She's even worse now, threatening to call the cops on you for kidnapping."

"I thought she kicked you out. Are you still there?"

"No, I'm at the condo in Northglenn."

"Isn't that place empty? As in no furniture?"

"I bought an air mattress," my dad replied, sounding defeated.

"We'll be back in a few days. Gianna just needs some time away from her mom."

"Where are you staying?"

I trusted my dad to a point, but Julie was relentless. Instead of answering him, I evaded the question. "Don't worry, everything's fine. I'm really sorry about you and Julie, dad."

"It's not really your fault, Caleb. You can't help who you fall in love with."

"I didn't say-"

He cut off my protest, "You didn't have to. I've been there twice before."

I ignored his comment, thinking him totally wrong.

After my moment of silence, he cleared his throat. "You know, yesterday I saw a side of Julie I'd never seen before. I didn't like it, Caleb. I love her, but if she has the ability to be so ugly towards my son and so easily throw away what we have, I'm not sure she's the right woman for me."

Hallelujah! Instead of praising the heavens above, I solemnly told him, "Sorry, dad."

"So, what should I tell her about Gianna next time she calls?"

"Just tell her this is us showing her she won't be able to keep us apart."

"That may not go over so well, Caleb. I'll try talking to her reasonably about it. I'm sure she's mostly worried about her daughter's wellbeing at this point. Assuring her Gianna is fine should help calm her some." My dad added hastily, "A phone call from Gianna wouldn't hurt."

"That's up to Gianna. Look, I have to go, I'm driving right now."

"Call me soon, Caleb."

"Will do."

I tossed my phone onto the seat and glanced at Gianna. She had a satisfied smile on her face. "What are you so happy about?"

"You," she said, leaning over to give me a peck on the cheek.

Okay, whatever.

By mid-afternoon, we were checking into a room at the Bellagio. Thank god for fake ids. When we got to the room, Gianna laid down for a nap. She wanted to be well rested for her first night in Vegas.

Sitting against the headboard as she slept beside me, I flipped through the channels. Tonight should be interesting. I came here with Dante and a couple other guys last summer. I had a feeling this trip was going to go a little differently. This time I'd only be having sex with one girl. In the past, that would've been a bad thing. Not so much now. But how long could that last? I was too young for this to be forever.

But it wouldn't be ending anytime soon. We hadn't even had sex yet. It did seem our relationship had come to that point. Gianna had indicated she was ready. I was way past ready. Was I supposed to tell her I loved her first? Would that make it more special for her? Do I even love her a little? I loved *being* with her, that was for sure. I'd been avoiding looking too deeply into my emotions where Gianna was concerned.

With love came complications neither of us needed. From what I'd seen of love, all it did was make people miserable. My parents were miserable together and now things were crashing and burning in my dad's relationship with Julie. Everyone ended up miserable when love was involved. I cared about Gianna more than anybody and anything else in the world. If I told her that, would it be enough?

Damn! A part of me wished she'd already had sex with someone else so there'd be less pressure on me. Of course, a bigger part of me would want to punch that nonexistent guy in the face. The entire situation sucked. I wanted to do this right. Unfortunately, this was my first real relationship and my examples of other relationships were all failures.

Gianna was right when she said I was nervous about having sex with her. I'd fucked up in life so much and this was the first time the thought of fucking up bothered me.

*****

As we were getting ready to go out, Gianna teased me that I actually managed to pack suitable clubbing clothes and shoes for her. It was definitely pure luck because I hadn't been paying attention in my packing frenzy.

Before leaving the room, I pulled my sexy girl in for a kiss. "You look beautiful, Gianna. Almost as hot as I do."

She rolled her eyes, smiling. "You are so full of yourself, Caleb."

"And by the end of the night, you'll be so full of me, too."

Gianna let out a sound that sounded like a mix between a laugh and a cough. She recovered and quickly changed the subject. "Number eight is only half completed. Let's go find a cool club and then I think we can officially call it accomplished."

I let her change of topic slide. "Okay. Let's go, party girl."

CHAPTER TWO

"Love is a game that two can play and both win."
-Eva Gabor

GIANNA

Caleb and I took a taxi over to the Palms casino to check out one of the clubs there. Caleb had heard of a club called *Rain* was supposed to be pretty cool. Even though it was a weeknight, the place was packed. Vegas probably never had a slow night.

I planned on not getting too drunk tonight. Caleb wasn't the type to have sex with a girl who was wasted. We got our drinks first and found an empty booth for some privacy. Caleb waited patiently for me to finish my drink then we headed out to the dance floor.

Caleb was so cute and protective, pushing his way through the crowd of people while holding my hand and dragging me along behind him. I was a little tipsy from the rush of alcohol and giggled. Part of me suspected he wanted to make sure no guys bumped into me while trying to cop a feel.

I hadn't forgotten the whole disagreement about who would be begging who by the end of the night. Caleb may have been the expert on sexual relationships, but I was still the female here. Virgin or not, I still held most of the power. They didn't call it pussy-whipped for nothing.

Although, Caleb seemed like the type of guy who could made a girl dick-whipped. I burst out in laughter and Caleb shook his head at me, making me abruptly stop as he grabbed my ass.

I was tired of him being so hesitant to have sex with me because I was a virgin. He'd given me enough innuendos about what he wanted to do to me, but hadn't followed through with any of them yet. I still remembered when he found out my v-card had yet to be punched and treated me like I carried a freaking disease.

When dancing to a sexy hip hop song, I made sure to rub against him a lot. My hand *accidentally* brushed against his crotch area.

My bad.

Caleb pulled my body even tighter against his own. I could almost see the hormones in the air, floating with the sensual beats of the music.

After dancing a few songs, we got more drinks and leaned against a railing since our former table was now occupied, along with all the others. The club was even more packed now than when we'd arrived. Sucking down the last of the alcohol at the bottom of my glass, I handed my drink to a passing waitress and shouted in Caleb's ear, "Don't get too drunk! I don't want to feel like I'm taking advantage of you later tonight!"

With him looking at me from the corner of his eye while tipping his drink back, I got the impression he was thinking some very naughty thoughts. The tight feeling low in my stomach was accompanied by heat in my cheeks. I was glad the club was dark so he couldn't laugh at my blush. Crap, I should've kept in mind what a big manwhore Caleb was. He was batting in the big leagues when playing this game while I was still benched in little league.

Deciding to quit while I was not exactly ahead, but neck and neck, I dragged him back to the dance floor. The DJ started a Black Eyed Peas track and I could totally relate to the song. I had a feeling tonight would be a good night, also.

The last drink began to hit me and I got my nerve back enough to tease Caleb some more on the dance floor. With my back to him, I rubbed against his front. Kind of like a bear scratching his back against a tree but with more hip movement. Hopefully this bear wouldn't bite too hard. Caleb's body began responding to mine and it was a good thing my back was to him otherwise he'd have seen my satisfaction.

Using his forearm to pull me back, he held me tightly against his chest. I could feel his breath against my ear as he shouted, "What are you doing, bad girl?"

I turned my head to the side against his shoulder to shout back in his ear, "Dancing!"

Then, right there on the dance floor, Caleb slipped his hands underneath the hem of my flimsy dress. The warmth of his palms rested on the front of my upper thighs, his index fingers teased my panty line. I scowled at him in accusation. His *What, who me?* innocent look wasn't fooling me.

I decided to call his bluff and outdo him. Flipping around, I pressed my hand firmly against the hard-on in his pants. Now it was his turn to look surprised. The shock quickly morphed into a heavy-lidded expression.

His hands were now gliding up the back of my thighs and over my butt cheeks left bare by my g-string. Even though his actions were making me hotter for him, I managed to keep a straight face. My flirtatious smile let him know I wasn't scared or backing down.

Not getting the scandalized reaction he wanted from me, he moved one hand between our bodies to cup me between my legs. Then the rubbing commenced. *Holy crap.* I closed my eyes at the sensations running through me. Upon opening my eyes, it was to see Caleb's smug smile.

Oh, hell no! The battle had just begun. Licking my lips, I yelled over the music while running a finger over his erection, "I want to taste you!"

As a shudder vibrated through his body, I could almost hear his groan. After closing his eyes for a moment, probably to imagine me at his knees, he recovered enough to say, "I want to hear you beg for it with that sweet little mouth of yours."

Wow, that was hot. His words almost had me wanting that exact scenario.

Pushing my immense lust for him aside, I focused on the ultimate goal. "You'll be the one begging before the night is over!"

His knowing smile made me nervous.

Like a light bulb, or maybe a strobe light, turning on above my head, an idea came to me. After all, this was Vegas, baby.

"Hey, Caleb!"

"Hey, Gianna!" he mocked me.

"Do you want a lap dance?"

He gave me a dirty look. "You're not playing nice!"

My arms tightened around his neck. "I can make it real *nice* for you." With my lips to his neck, I ran kisses up to the back of his ear. "Your own personal stripper."

Caleb was practically squeezing my body at that point. My guy liked my bright idea. I giggled against his neck. "You are so asking for it, princess."

"Promises, promises!" I teased him.

Without warning, he pivoted us and guided me off the dance floor toward the exit. Okay, I guess we were leaving. Maybe I was about to be punished for testing him.

Once out in front of the hotel, Caleb guided me into a cab. He told the driver to take us to the nearest convenience store and pulled me onto his lap as the driver took off. I laughed at his eagerness.

"What's so funny, Gianna?"

"You are. I almost have you begging for it."

Caleb nuzzled my neck. "The night isn't over yet, sexy girl."

"What's that supposed to mean?"

"It means, when we get back to the hotel room, I'm going to have you begging me to fuck you." Caleb did an impression of my voice for his next words. "Harder, Caleb! Please, Caleb, make me come again!"

Dammit, I'd never even had sex and he was making me want to beg for it already. *Stay strong, Gianna.* Pussy-whipped, not dick-whipped was the ultimate goal.

"Lap dance," I taunted him.

"My mouth between your legs," he taunted me back.

I cocked my head to the side, not able to hold back my curiosity. "Will I like that?"

"You will when I do it." As if to give me a preview, his kissed me, stroking my tongue with his in a way that had me squirming on his lap.

The cab driver coughed and I remembered our audience of one. Whatever, he worked in Las Vegas, he could deal with a makeout session in the back of his dirty cab. We stopped at a gas station and Caleb asked the driver to wait for us.

He ushered me through the sliding doors of the gas station with a hand at my back. The place seemed a little skeevy, but busy. Every gas pump outside was being put to use and there was a line in front of both cash registers.

"What are we here for?"

"Supplies," Caleb replied vaguely.

Holding my hand, he dragged me over to the condoms. I glanced around, thinking this was a position I'd never really thought of being in. The speed at which he immediately grabbed a box had me thinking about how many times he'd likely bought that particular brand. At the coolers in the back of the store he handed me a four pack of wine coolers and picked a six pack of beer for himself. Girly wine coolers for me and manly beer for him, typical guy.

Standing in line to pay, I was sure we'd get busted at any moment and I'd end up in a jail cell with a hooker. We climbed back into the cab and I breathed a sigh of relief. No hooker roommate tonight. Caleb asked the driver to take us to the Bellagio. I was back in Caleb's lap as we cruised down the strip, having to stop at red lights occasionally for pedestrians to cross the street.

"Hey, Caleb?" I got his attention while running my hands through his silky dark hair.

"Yes?"

"How do you have so much money?" I asked him, voicing the question for the first time after wondering for awhile.

The cautious look in his eyes had me pressing on. "Well, this whole trip is costing a lot of money. Where did you get it from? Did you work a summer job or something? I was just wondering why you always seem to have money."

He shifted uncomfortably at my questioning and, instead of answering, directed a question back at me. "Why do *you* always have money?"

Hmm, I'd let it go for now. "We've never talked about it, but my dad is a plastic surgeon in Houston. Besides paying child support to my mom each month, he deposits a hefty allowance into my bank account. He knows how controlling my mom can be, so he wants me to have that freedom."

Caleb looked amused. "So you're a daddy's girl?"

"Yes," I answered, unashamed. "My dad is always trying to get me to move with him to Houston. He wants Chance with him, also, but knows my mom has more free time to spend with him. I wouldn't want to ever leave my friends in the crew, anyways."

"Why doesn't he move here, then?"

I gave him a skeptical look. "Would you? I mean, you've met my mom. He talked about moving back to Denver years ago after he finished his residency in Houston, but I'm sure my mom's psychotic behavior was what made him rethink it."

Caleb laughed and kissed my nose. "I see your point. Don't worry, she won't be able to drive me away."

I playfully yanked on his shirt. "You better not let her, or I'll come after you."

Getting out of the cab in front of our hotel, I remembered Caleb never answered my question about where he got his money from. I'd have to grill him on it later. We managed to get an elevator all to ourselves after a group of girls in tiny dresses unloaded from it. Caleb pulled me into his body as the doors shut.

Kissing me long and hard, he finally let me up for air. "Now, about that lap dance. . . ."

I purposely acted unsure. "I don't know, Caleb. How bad do you want it? Bad enough to *beg*?"

Caleb glared at me. "Woman, you will take off that dress and dance on my lap while rubbing your hot little body all over me."

We exited the elevator on the tenth floor and walked down the long carpeted hallway to our room. Outside our door, I pretended to think about it. "Um, no thanks."

Once inside the room he backed me against the wall, his body leaning into mine. "Come on, Gianna. You're killing me."

I tried to hold back a grin. "Do I hear begging coming on?"

Caleb groaned and dropped his head in defeat. When he raised it again, the evil look in his eyes was alarming. "Okay, I'll beg. For now." I had a feeling my win would be a short one. He ran his hands all over my body in a way that had me thinking being the loser wouldn't be so bad after all. His sexy voice drew me back from my erotic thoughts. "Gianna, you're making me so hot. Will you please, I'm begging you, *please* give me a lap dance?"

Hmm. Not the way I'd pictured his begging in my mind. It wasn't supposed to have me wanting to beg for more of that bedroom voice. But now it was time for me to follow through with my part of our deal.

"Alright," I said with heavy reluctance, like I was about to do a chore I detested. "Go sit in that chair over there, the one without the armrests."

The anticipation on his handsome face was funny. Like a little kid on Christmas morning. Caleb moved the chair to an open space and leaned back, waiting for the show to begin.

It suddenly hit me that I was no stripper and I could very possibly make a fool of myself. "One minute," I requested, practically running into the bathroom.

Gripping the counter, I mouthed, "Holy shit!" to myself in the mirror. Cece and I had signed up for a pole dancing class when we were fourteen but were forced to drop it before it started because of Jared's big mouth. Her mom had freaked and called the dance studio, telling them off for letting two "little girls" enroll. Therefore, I had no real stripper skills.

The thought suddenly hit me that my boyfriend had probably been to a strip club. Knowing him, he'd probably had at least one lap dance from some nasty skank. That meant he had something to compare me to, that I had competition. Some nameless, well her name had likely been something like Candy or Cherry, had rubbed her ass and tits all over my man and I needed to erase her from his memory.

My nervousness didn't matter anymore. Grabbing my makeup bag, I dug through it for my red lipstick. As I carefully applied it to my lips, I channeled my inner sex kitten. It took some digging, but she was there. Coming awake, she stretched her limbs seductively and smirked, awaiting my direction.

Okay, I could do this.

Opening the bathroom door, I heard the music Caleb had playing on his phone. Rihanna, *perfect*. The room was lit by a single lamp but the curtains were open to let in the lights from the strip. His eyes rested on me as I moved closer. In my head, I was choreographing the performance ahead.

Walking to where he sat, instead of stopping in front of him as expected, I circled around the chair, running my fingers through his hair. I gave his hair a little tug before letting go as I stopped in front of Caleb with my back to him at the exact spot the glow of Vegas coming through the window.

I slowly unzipped the side of my dress, letting it fall down my arms and over my hips as they swayed to the music. The dress dropped to the floor, leaving me in only my bra and panties. Nothing he hadn't seen before.

The song changed to one of Usher's and I spun around while running my hands up my neck and lifting my hair. Caleb eyed my lace panties like he was wishing for x-ray vision. Not that they left a lot to the imagination.

I gave him a stern look. "No touching the talent."

He raised his eyebrows, not exactly agreeing to the rule. Straddling him, I started moving my hips, dancing seductively while grinding my crotch against his. Why had I been freaking out earlier? I loved this!

Caleb lifted his hands in the air like he was about to grab my waist, but I slapped them away. Maybe I should've had mercy on him, but this was too much fun. I ran my hands over his shirt from his chest to his stomach, stopping short of where he wanted them most.

Turning around, with my legs spread out on either side of his, I continued to grind on his lap. Caleb cleared his throat. "Usually strippers only wear panties. Time to lose the bra."

I looked back at him with a scowl. "Had many lap dances, have you?"

Caleb suddenly found the ceiling more interesting than the half-naked chick on his lap. "A few."

I sighed, already guessing but not liking having it confirmed. "I guess I won't be your first anything, will I?"

Caleb smiled and leaned his face into my hair. "No, but you can be my best." Whether that was true or not, it was a sweet thing to say.

Which of course earned him bra removal.

I took it off, holding my arms over my breasts, glancing back at him with an innocent expression. "Want me to turn around again?"

"Now," he demanded forcefully.

"No," I pouted.

The desire and lust in his eyes both thrilled and scared me. "That's it. I'm touching what's mine." He reached around me to push my arms down and palm both of my breasts.

"Caleb!" I gasped out then moaned when he flicked my nipples with his thumbs.

"You like?" He whispered in my ear, licking along my neck.

I managed to nod. Actually, I liked it a lot.

When the song changed again, I resumed dancing and arching my back against him, but at a faster pace. With my back still against his chest and his hands still holding onto my breasts, I was feeling the music like never before.

Caleb grabbed onto my hair to pull my head back. "Gianna," he hissed in my ear, "You're way too good at this. You haven't done it for any guy before me, have you?"

I shook my head. "Never. Swear."

"Good because you're mine." He reached down with one hand, sliding it into the front of my g-string. Two fingers entering me made me groan. The foreign feeling was far from unwelcome. "You're so wet for me."

Caleb began fingering me, making me pant for more. "Oh god, Caleb, that feels so amazing."

"You want more?" He leaned back in his chair, grinding me against his crotch while pushing his fingers in and out of me slowly. The dancing was forgotten as pleasure took over.

I felt like I was on the verge of something spectacular, but it wasn't quite enough to throw me over the edge. "Caleb, more."

"Do you want me inside you?" Caleb whispered in my ear, gently biting my earlobe.

"*Yes.*"

"You have to beg for it, Gianna."

I didn't even care about my pride anymore. "Please Caleb, please?"

"Please what, Gianna?" Caleb was enjoying torturing me.

"Please can I have you inside me?"

I felt Caleb's rumbling growl where my back met his chest. It turned me on more. He stood, picking me up in the process. "I have to fuck you right now."

Sounded like someone wanted it as badly as I did.

He laid me down on the bed and started undressing himself. His shoes flew across the room, followed by his pants and shirt. Standing there in his black boxer briefs, staring down at me, was the guy who set me on fire at the same time he made me melt. "Jesus Christ, Gianna, I wanted to go slowly with you the first time, but I don't think I can."

"Give it to me however you want, just hurry. I need you now, Caleb."

Hooking his thumbs in my panties, he slipped them off, licking his lips in the process. He spread my knees slowly while his gaze burned into mine. As his eyes moved from my face to between my legs, I could swear they began to glow in appreciation. Kneeling before the bed, he pulled me closer to the edge. I gasped in both surprise and arousal as his mouth descended. After one leisurely lick, he began devouring me.

Holy Crap that felt great.

"Caleb! Oh god, Caleb! Oh god!" Coherent thought had been discarded along with my panties.

Caleb suddenly stood up to get rid of his boxer briefs, making me whimper in protest. I spied a tattoo low on his stomach, but didn't have time to get a good look before he was moving over me, positioning his lower body between my legs. So, he did really have a tattoo down there.

Caleb stroked my face, giving me a kiss so passionate it conveyed the extreme lust he felt for me. I attempted to answer his message with one of my own. When I opened my eyes, his face held a more tender emotion than before. Girly butterflies fluttered in my stomach.

Any lingering doubts about giving my virginity to Caleb flew out the window and into the flashy Vegas night.

Holding my gaze, he thrusted into me, stopping to hold himself still. I communicated the pain with a yelp and a death grip on his shoulders. He gently smoothed out the hair over my forehead. "Shh, it's okay, baby. It's better to get it over with fast. It'll pass."

He was right, the pain was already fading, leaving behind a fullness.

"What about a condom?" I reminded him.

He sucked his bottom lip in, looking torn. "I wear a condom with every other girl, but not with you. I want to be able to feel you the first time."

My smile was shy, not knowing what to say to all that. "It doesn't hurt anymore."

Caleb kissed me again, starting to slowly rock in and out of me. "Gianna," he groaned, "you feel so damn good." He his eyes were squeezed shut and the tortured ecstasy on his face made me hotter.

With his forearms braced on either side of me, only his lower body weight was pressing down on me. I got up on my elbows to lift my mouth and suck on one of his pierced nipples. He groaned, using one hand to grip the back of my head while thrusting harder and faster.

He let go of my head to rest his other forearm against the bed again. I fell back against the mattress. "Caleb, you feel so good inside me. We should've done this sooner. Like the day we met."

He let out a strangled laugh and smiled down at me. "Like that, huh?"

"Love it."

"Then you'll really love this," he promised, then repositioned both of us so he was on his knees and a pillow was beneath me, lifting me up for him. His thrusts felt deeper now as he rubbed between my legs with his thumb. His other hand gripped my hip to keep me in place.

It.

Was.

Incredible.

A sensation was building low in my stomach before bursting into a climax that had my back arching and my brain scrambling.

"Caleb, I love you," I moaned, feeling more than I'd ever felt at one time in my life.

The afterglow was accompanied by a feeling of relaxation and contentment which had me closing my eyes and resting my head to the side.

When I opened my eyes and turned my head forward, I saw Caleb leaning over me with an intense look on his face. The fuzziness cleared as I realized what I'd just said.

Caleb opened his mouth and hesitated before saying. "Gianna, I. . . ." He swallowed, with a panicked look in his eyes.

Not wanting anything to ruin the moment, I cupped his cheek with my hand. "It's okay. You don't have to say it back."

I already knew his feelings ran deep for me. I could be patient and wait until he was ready to say the words.

He was about to say something else, maybe something that should be left unsaid, so I leaned up and kissed him to shut him up. I didn't want him to say anything we'd both regret. He was still hard inside me, which at least made me feel better. My declaration hadn't been a turnoff for him. Caleb kept kissing me as he continued to make love to me. Minutes later, he groaned my name against my lips as he climaxed.

His harsh breathing was warm against my neck where he rested his face. Popping his head up, he gave me a grin. "Yep, definitely the best."

Gianna gets a gold star.

I smiled lazily at him. "For me, too."

He laughed arrogantly, probably proud he was my first. I was glad I had no one to compare him to. It made being with him all the more special.

Danger! Bad Boy

He pulled out and wrapped me in his arms, draping one leg over mine as he covered us with the bedding. "You better get some rest, Gianna, because I may be waking you up in the middle of the night for round two."

I dozed off, but woke up soon after when I felt him unwrap himself from around me. He came back a minute later with a wet washcloth. I opened my eyes to see him drawing back the blanket to gently clean up between my legs. Closing my eyes with a sigh, I fell into a deep sleep.

CHAPTER THREE

"Love is a friendship se .
                              -Joseph Campu .

REWIND - CHAPTER TWO FROM CALEB'S PERSPECTIVE

CALEB

Gianna and I left our hotel and took a taxi to the Palms Casino to check out club Rain. I'd been to Vegas a couple times, but never to this particular club. It was supposed to be pretty hot.

Tonight would be interesting, given our little game of who would beg first. *Stay strong*, I told myself. I didn't want to look like a freaking loser, begging my girlfriend for sex.

Once we were in the club, we went to the bar first. I got a beer for myself and a Long Island Iced Tea for Gianna. Girls always loved that drink.

I finished my beer and waited patiently while Gianna drank the last of her drink. It was time to see my girl shake it on the dance floor. I grabbed Gianna's hand and led her through the thick crowd. I made sure to throw warning looks at any guys who checked her out. Guys always thought being at a club where girls wore skimpy clothing gave them a license to act like pervs.

I was eager to finally have sex with her. My dry spell would be coming to an end tonight. Staking my claim was how I saw it. I'd try to be as romantic as I could about it. But like Gianna always pointed out, I was no expert at hearts and flowers. God, I didn't want to fuck this up. If I played my cards right, I'd have Gianna begging before, during and after. All of my manwhore experience would finally be put to good use.

Damn, though, I was nervous about it being her first time. It almost always hurt the first time for virgins. One of the many reasons I'd sworn to steer clear of them. The bad experiences were legendary. I shuddered at the thought of Gianna's first time being anything but pleasurable.

The DJ changed the track to a hip hop song, giving Gianna the excuse to rub herself up on me. Not that I was complaining. Gianna's hand brushed against my already hard dick and I couldn't tell if she did it on purpose or not. I was horny as hell. Grabbing onto her hips, I pulled her body closer to mine.

We danced for awhile before going back to the bar to get more drinks. Finding a spot by a railing, we managed to drink them without getting bumped into by people. The place had to be filled to maximum capacity.

I was almost done with my beer when Gianna leaned over to shout in my ear, "Don't get too drunk! I don't want to feel like I'm taking advantage of you later tonight!"

Not likely.

I laughed at her comment and gave her the kind of look that let her know just how impossible it would be for her to take advantage of me. Images of all the ways I'd fuck her flashed through my mind. The expression on her face told me she'd read me loud and clear.

Gianna finished her second drink and tugged on my hand to lead me to the dance floor. Someone sure enjoyed rubbing against my body. A Black Eyed Peas song was playing. The lyrics made me laugh. I had a feeling, too, down in my pants.

I could tell the liquor was affecting Gianna because she was dancing even sexier than before. Her back was to me and she was rubbing her ass all over my crotch. I couldn't see her face, but my eyes narrowed and I was suspicious she was teasing me on purpose. Trying to get a rise out of a certain part of me.

I wrapped my arms around her chest from behind and pulled her in tight. Shouting in her ear over the music, I asked, "What are you doing, bad girl?"

She turned her head to shout back at me, "Dancing!"

I could hear the laughter in her voice. Two could play at that game. I was the master, after all. The poor girl didn't stand a chance.

The dance floor was packed, so I felt it was relatively safe to do a little teasing of my own. Her back was still to my chest when I reached down and slipped my hand underneath her dress. At first I simply touched her thighs and had to hold back my laughter at the look of shock she threw at me. My finger ran along the edge of her panties and she shivered. I gave her my most innocent look.

She whipped around so she was facing me and grabbed onto my dick through my pants.

Holy motherfucking crap!

Pull yourself together, Caleb. Not the first time a girl grabbed your junk.

I decided to enjoy her boldness, letting her know from my expression how much I loved the attention. Besides, two could play at that game.

My hands were now on the back of her thighs, so I slid them up to cup her butt cheeks. She was wearing a g-string. *Nice.* She squirmed a little, but kept a calm look on her face. Naïve girl thought she still had a chance at winning. Her naughty smile tempted me more than anything else.

Gianna obviously forgot who she was messing with. *Time to teach the little tease a lesson.* I moved one hand between our bodies and rubbed her pussy through her panties. Her eyes closed almost immediately and her head dropped against my chest.

When she pulled her head back and met my gaze, I didn't bother wiping the satisfied smile off my face. Her glare had me shaking with laughter.

Lightly rubbing my dick with one finger, she put her lips to my ear and yelled, "I want to taste you!"

I shuddered in anticipation at the thought, hornier than before. As she bit her lip, I glanced at her mouth, thinking of all the fun coming my way.

Girl didn't even want to try matching my skills at talking dirty. "I want to hear you beg for it with that sweet little mouth of yours."

She glared at me again but licked her lips. "You'll be the one begging before the night is over!"

I gave her a confident smile.

She got a mischievous look on her face. "Hey, Caleb!"

"Hey, Gianna!" I teased her.

"Do you want a lap dance?" Her grin was triumphant.

And just like that, she found my kryptonite.

"You're not playing fair!"

She wrapped her arms snugly around my neck, pressing her breasts against my chest. "I can make it real *nice* for you." Dropping kisses, her lips ran from my neck to ear to further tempt me. "Your own personal stripper."

Liking her in my arms and loving how she thought, I squeezed her body tightly. Her giggle was adorable. She mistakenly assumed she finally had the upper hand. I pressed my lips against her ear. "You are so asking for it, princess."

"Promises, promises!" she said playfully.

That's it!

Snatching her up off the ground, I quickly turned her towards the exit before setting her back down. Placing an arm around the back of her waist, I guided her off the dance floor and out of the club.

Life was good when you were about to get laid.

We left the hotel and I practically threw her into a cab. I asked the cab driver to take us to the nearest convenience store and pulled Gianna onto my lap. She laughed, still thinking she had the upper hand. She didn't realize that all lessons taught tonight were going to be by me.

"What's so funny, Gianna?"

"You are. I almost have you begging for it." Her smug smile made me want to laugh.

Instead, I nuzzled her neck. "The night isn't over yet, sexy girl."

"What's that supposed to mean?" she questioned suspiciously.

"It means, when we get back to the hotel room, I'm going to have you begging me to fuck you," I told her, then added in a high-pitched girly voice, "Harder, Caleb! Please, Caleb, make me come again!"

I couldn't wait to hear her climax while moaning my name.

"Lap dance," she said in a taunting voice.

"My mouth between your legs," I said in a similar tone.

Tilting her head to the side, she looked thoughtful. "Will I like that?"

"You will when I do it." I had the utmost confidence in my abilities. Depending on the girl, I didn't always go down on her during sex. If a girl was a nasty slut, I had no interest in licking passed around pussy. Any other time, I usually enjoyed what was on offer.

To show Gianna what was in store for her, I kissed her deeply.

The cab driver coughed and I ignored his uptight ass. However, I didn't want him getting any ideas about my girl. Another guy even thinking about her in a sexual way would piss me off big time. Gianna was a good girl.

And all mine.

We stopped at a gas station and I asked the driver to wait for us. As we went inside, Gianna asked, "What are we here for?"

"Supplies," I informed her. I grabbed a box of condoms and some alcohol. Beer for me and strawberry wine coolers for her. *Hmm, strawberry kisses from Gianna.*

After waiting in line to pay, we got back into the cab and told the driver to take us back to our hotel. I pulled Gianna back onto my lap again. Right where she belonged. With all the people walking the strip, traffic was slow moving. I didn't mind, the anticipation would make it all the sweeter.

"Hey, Caleb?" Gianna asked, her graceful fingers in my hair.

"Yes?"

"How do you have so much money?" Her question caught me off guard.

I ignored her question, but in typical girl fashion, she didn't let it go. "Well, this whole trip is costing a lot of money. Where did you get it from? Did you work a summer job or something? I was just wondering why you always seem to have money."

Damn, how to answer? How about not at all? I turned the question on her. "Why do *you* always have money?"

Her expression was both knowing and frustrated, but she answered anyway. "We've never talked about it, but my dad is a plastic surgeon in Houston. Besides paying child support to my mom each month, he deposits a hefty allowance into my bank account He knows how controlling my mom can be, so he wants me to have that freedom."

Plus, the guy probably felt guilty about leaving her with crazy Julie.

"So you're a daddy's girl?" I teased her, figuring with such a pretty daughter, her dad couldn't resist spoiling her.

"Yes," she admitted like she was proud of it. "My dad is always trying to get me to move with him to Houston. He wants Chance with him, also, but knows my mom has more free time to spend with him. I wouldn't want to ever leave my friends in the crew, anyways."

"Why doesn't he move here then?" I asked. No way did I want her moving to Houston.

She looked at me as if I were crazy. "Would you? I mean, you've met my mom. He talked about moving back to Denver years ago after he finished his residency in Houston, but my I'm sure my mom's psychotic behavior is what made him rethink it."

I laughed, unable to resist kissing the tip of her nose. "I see your point. Don't worry, she won't be able to drive me away."

She tried to act intimidating by grabbing onto my shirt. "You better not let her, or I'll come after you."

All she accomplished was to make me think of rough sex. Which she unfortunately wouldn't be ready for the first couple times.

I'd successfully managed to evade her earlier question. Hopefully it wouldn't come up again. She may not like the answer. Truthfully, she definitely wouldn't like the answer.

When we were alone on the elevator, I pulled her into my arms and kissed her to let her know my mood hadn't changed. "Now, about that lap dance. . . ."

She pretended to act unsure. "I don't know, Caleb. How bad do you want it? Bad enough to *beg*?"

Hot little bitch didn't know when to quit.

I decided to take charge and gave her a hard look. "Woman, you will take off that dress and dance on my lap while rubbing your hot little body all over me."

She remained silent as we got off the elevator on the tenth floor and walked down the hallway to our room. Outside of our door, she finally replied, "Um, no thanks."

Too late, she'd already offered. There was no taking it back now.

As soon as the hotel room door closed, I pushed her up against the wall, my body trapping hers. "Come on, Gianna. You're killing me."

She looked so cute with that smug grin on her face, thinking she'd won. "Do I hear a beg coming on?"

I groaned and put my head down, as if defeated. I knew I had a mischievous smile on my face when I lifted my head back up to look at her. "Okay, I'll beg. For now." Her eyes went wide. I ran my hands up and down her body then said in a voice sure to make her wet if she wasn't already, "Gianna, you're making me so hot. Will you please, I'm begging you, *please* give me a lap dance?"

I saw apprehension flash through her eyes before she replied with fake reluctance, "Alright."

I could tell she'd lost some of her confidence, but I wasn't going to tease her about it and make her uncomfortable or ruin my chances of getting her naked on my lap.

"Go sit in that chair over there, the one without the armrests."

This was going to be awesome.

"One minute," she squeaked, disappearing into the bathroom.

Looking through my phone, I found a Rihanna song about sex. I adjusted the room until only a single lamp was on. The view of the Vegas strip through the open curtains was a reminder we were in Sin City. Inhibitions were abandoned at the city limits.

My eyes on the bathroom door, I was seated and ready when she came out.

Coming towards me, instead of stepping between my legs where I wanted her, she went around me, running her fingers through my hair. She yanked my hair gently and finally moved to my front. Her back was to me as she slowly unzipped the side of her dress and peeled it down her body, letting it fall to the floor. The striptease was done to the gentle beat of the music.

Damn, she looked so hot in just her bra and panties. She hadn't stopped dancing and when the next song on the playlist began, one of Usher's, she spun around. The way she touched her hips, her neck, lifted up her hair, had me wanting to jump out of the chair and throw her on the bed. Lace lingerie was a good look on her. Her cleavage was insane.

Her expression turned serious. "No touching the talent."

My raised eyebrows let her know what I thought of that. Things only improved when she straddled me. Her pussy grinding against my dick as she moved her hips practically had my eyes rolling to the back of my head. Best lap dance ever.

I was about to grab onto her waist when she slapped my hands. I forgave her when she began touching my chest and stomach. Then I was annoyed all over again when her hands went no further south.

Forgiveness was once again hers when she reversed her position with her legs spread out over mine. I couldn't decide if her pussy or her ass rubbing against me was my favorite.

Clearing my throat, I informed her, "Usually strippers only wear panties. Time to lose the bra."

She turned her head back with a scowl on those pretty lips. "Had many lap dances, have you?"

I'd walked right into that one. Avoiding her eyes, I answered almost guiltily, "A few."

She sighed, making me think of other sounds she'd be making tonight. "I guess I won't be your first anything, will I?"

Leaning my face into her hair, I decided I liked her jealousy. As long as she was spreading her legs for me, she could be possessive over my dick. "No, but you can be my best."

And I'd be her only. That thought had me feeling possessive myself.

I must have chosen the right thing to say because off went the bra.

With her arms crossed over her breasts, she glanced back at me with an angelic look on her beautiful face. "Want me to turn around again?"

"Now," I ordered her.

"No," she pouted the word, her lips forming a small circle.

The girl was driving me crazy. I wanted to pin her down and pound into her. "That's it. I'm touching what's mine." Reaching around, I slapped her arms down and cupped her tits.

Fucking perfect.

"Caleb!" she gasped my name, moaning as my thumbs played with her nipples.

"You like?" I whispered in her ear, licking her neck, enjoying the taste of her skin.

Gianna nodded jerkily. My girl was horny.

The song switched to hip hop and she arched and swayed on my lap at a faster pace. With my hands on her tits, she seemed even more into the dancing. Everything about her was sexy, her ass bared by the g-string, her naked back and the way she relished my touch.

I was getting off on the power I had over her. It felt like the high of ownership. Jealousy surged through me as I remembered the time I found her dancing seductively to a Shakira song in front of Jared while they were camping and partying. Gripping her hair, I gently pulled her head back. "Gianna," I whispered harshly, "You're way too good at this. You haven't done it for any guy before me, have you?"

She shook her head despite my hand in her hair. "Never. Swear."

"Good because you're mine." I slipped a hand into the front of her panties. Wetness greeted the two fingers I slid into her. Her moan drove me to continue. "You're so wet for me."

No other guy had touched her pussy either.

She squirmed in my lap as I fingered her. "Oh god, Caleb, that feels so amazing."

"You want more?" Leaning back, I had one hand on her hip and the other at her pussy and used both grips to grind her ass back against my dick. She'd stopped dancing, but it didn't matter anymore. The real games had begun.

Gianna's breaths were short and she was moving against my fingers. In a way, it was a different kind of dance. "Caleb, more."

"Do you want me inside you?" I asked her, lightly pulling her earlobe between my teeth.

"*Yes*," she answered, but I wanted her gagging for it.

"You have to beg for it, Gianna."

There was no hesitation on her part. "Please, Caleb, please?"

"Please what, Gianna?" She was beginning to learn who was in control.

"Please can I have you inside me?"

Her pleading was so sweet. It made me feel like dirtying her up, doing nasty things to her.

With a growl, I stood up, taking her with me. "I have to fuck you right now."

I placed her on the bed, barely refraining from tossing her. I took off everything but my underwear. Looking down at her, I couldn't believe this gorgeous girl was all mine. She wasn't covering her breasts and I drank in the sight of them. "Jesus Christ, Gianna, I wanted to go slowly with you the first time, but I don't think I can."

"Give it to me however you want, just hurry. I need you now, Caleb."

Wanting to tear off her panties, I managed to slide them down her legs. Hands on her knees, I spread them as I looked into her eyes. Savoring the moment, I moved my gaze down until I saw the prettiest pussy ever. I dragged her closer to the edge of the bed and swooped down for my first taste.

Taking my time at first, I couldn't hold back for long.

"Caleb! Oh god, Caleb! Oh god!" She was going crazy as I enjoyed her.

Feeling at my limit, I yanked down my boxer briefs as she whimpered at the pause in festivities. I got on the bed over her, relishing finally being between her legs.

Touching her face, I kissed her with everything I was feeling. Along with being more aroused than I could remember, my chest felt tight. She returned my kiss with a matched eagerness. Looking down at her, my emotions were in a jumble.

At the forefront was the urge to make her mine. Her blue eyes gazed trustingly into mine as I entered her, stopping at the one thrust to let her get used to me. With a small cry of pain, she was holding onto my shoulders. Pushing her hair off her forehead, I told her, "Shh, it's okay, baby. It's better to get it over with fast. It'll pass."

Damn, she was tight.

"What about a condom?" she asked worriedly.

It was unbelievable that I'd forgotten, it'd never happened with the girls before her. Knowing she was right, but feeling primal, I couldn't bring myself to put one on. "I wear a condom with every other girl, but not with you. I want to be able to feel you the first time."

To me, this was more real than any other experience I'd had.

Her small smile was encouraging. "It doesn't hurt anymore."

Not wanting to rush her, I thrusted slowly in and out. "Gianna," I groaned, "you feel so damn good." My eyes closed at the tight grip she had on me.

I could get addicted to this pussy.

I braced my upper body up with my forearms, making sure to only put my lower body weight on her. Before I realized what she was doing, my nipple was in her mouth, piercing and all. Holding the back of her head, I kept her where she was. Uncontrollably, I began pumping in and out of her harder.

Not that she was complaining.

Releasing her, she fell back onto the bed with flushed cheeks. "Caleb, you feel so good inside me. We should've done this sooner. Like the day we met."

My laugh sounded tortured. "Like that, huh?"

"Love it."

"Then you'll really love this," I assured her, repositioning her with pillows beneath her as I got up on my knees. Rubbing her clit, I pounded deeper into her. Holding her in place with my other hand, I realized no girl had come close to feeling this good.

She was moaning and panting, getting closer to release. I watched as her back arched off the bed as she climaxed, making the hottest sound I'd ever heard. At the end of her orgasm she moaned words that rocked me, "Caleb, I love you."

Gianna's eyes were still closed and I wasn't sure she realized what she'd said. Her eyelids lifted slowly and suddenly wider.

I opened my mouth to say I don't know what. All that came out was, "Gianna, I. . . ." Feeling on the spot, I couldn't think of anything else. I was frustrated, nervous and bizarrely elated at the concept of her loving me.

She wasn't the first girl to tell me she loved me, but she was the first girl who made me feel like I should say something back.

Before I could think any more on it, she placed her palm against my cheek. "It's okay. You don't have to say it back."

Relief rushed through me and I was happy to be let off the hook. However, I still felt like I should say something. This funny, sexy girl loved me. Somehow, I felt lucky. My thoughts scattered as she kissed me.

I was still making love to her and it got more incredible. My lips were on hers as I came. Groaning her name, I experienced a climax like none other.

My face was buried against her neck. Lifting my head, I returned her smile. "Yep, definitely the best."

She looked beyond content. "For me, too."

I laughed, satisfied. Being her first, of course I was the best. Suddenly, I had the insane urge to make sure I was her only.

I pulled out of her slowly and wrapped my arms around her. Hooking a leg over hers possessively, I covered us up with a blanket. "You better get some rest, Gianna, because I may be waking you up in the middle of the night for round two."

She was starting to fall asleep when I got out of bed and went into the bathroom to clean myself up. I wet a hotel washcloth and strode back to the bed. I drew back the blanket just enough to clean her up down there. Her eyes slit open but she laid there passively. The high of ownership was back, making me feel a little like an asshole.

She fell back to sleep as I covered up her hot body with the blanket. I looked down at the towel in my hand, tinged with a small amount of red.

Gazing down at Gianna, I realized nothing had ever been precious to me before. Now this beautiful girl had become the most precious and important thing in my world.

She'd told me she loved me. While her loving me made me cautiously happy, I wasn't sure what I had to offer her. I didn't ever want love any girl and I didn't think I could love her back like she wanted.

I witnessed firsthand the hell loving my dad was for my mom. In the end, he didn't love her back enough. The way he loved Julie wasn't right either. Look how easily she threw his love away.

If Gianna said it again, should I say it back if it was untrue? I was in no doubt that I cared a lot for her. I loved spending time with her and I liked everything about her. On top of that, she was the best fuck in all of my experiences.

I ran my fingers through my hair in frustration. This relationship stuff was hard. Being a player had been so simple. I just hit it and moved on to the next available pussy.

Things were more complicated now. The way I was feeling at that moment, I didn't think I'd ever want to move on from Gianna.

CHAPTER FOUR

"Love me when I least deserve it, because
that's when I really need it."
-Swedish Proverb

CALEB

I woke in the middle of the night with Gianna curled up against me. Her body was so soft and warm against mine. Even in her sleep, she was asking for it. At least, that was the excuse in my head for what I did next.

The bathroom door was cracked open, letting in just enough light to get a visual. I pulled the sheet back to get a look at her hot little body.

Easing her onto her back, she grumbled in her sleep. I ran my hands down her body until I reached her thighs, spreading them open to touch between her legs until she was wet for me. I knew I should be gentle with her, since she'd just lost her virginity a few hours ago.

Deciding to surprise her, I filled her slowly, causing her to finally wake up. "Caleb?" she murmured sleepily.

"Who else were you expecting?" I teased her.

I was holding still inside her, letting her get used to the intrusion. "What is this? Open season on my vagina?"

"Yours?" I asked in mock disbelief. "It's mine now."

She laughed, making her whole body shake. I groaned at the unintended sensations where we were connected.

Not able to hold back any longer, I began rocking in and out of her. Her legs wrapped around me, giving me a better angle. Grinding into her just right, I had her climaxing on a long moan. I liked hearing my name as she came, but with an unexpected pang of regret I missed the more tender words she'd said last time.

Deciding to shake it off, I drove into her harder until my orgasm had me seeing stars.

Fucking heaven.

As I pulled out, she curled to her side with an adorable little smile on her face. "Thank you," she sighed in contentment, already lowering her lids to return to slumber.

I chuckled, tucking her into me. "You're more than welcome. Sweet dreams, princess."

Her lids remained closed but she made a sour face. "No more waking me up."

I spanked her on the butt. "Go to sleep!"

"I am so kicking your ass when I wake up in ten hours." she muttered sulkily and drifted back to sleep.

Sitting up, I stared at her sleeping face. God, she really was the most beautiful girl I'd ever seen. After getting to know her, I tended to forget it. Her personality kept my interest beyond her looks.

She'd been unhappy when I'd first met her. Living a lie and playing a part she'd detested. Except for her crew. It seemed like I'd finally got Jared off our backs. He accepted our relationship, but that could just be him saving face. No doubt, in a heartbeat he'd be willing to take my place in Gianna's life.

I lightly stroked her full bottom lip with my thumb. She was my pretty girl, now. Jared wouldn't be getting the chance to take my place. No one would.

She was happy now with me. At least I'd put a smile on her face. But was it love? Why did it have to be? Why couldn't things stay the way they were now? In my opinion, we had an absolutely ideal relationship. We could continue to have fun, have loads of sex and not ruin it with love crap.

Perfection.

Closing my eyes and laying my head on the pillow next to hers, I figured Gianna and I would have to talk about our relationship in the morning. I'd explain my way of thinking to her and she'd understand. She'd see that my way would cause less hassle. Love inevitably beat relationships to death, killing the connection two people started out with.

Having the issue settled in my mind, I followed the girl in my arms into sleep.

GIANNA

Waking up to the feel of an unfamiliar weight across my chest, I slowly opened my eyes. The sunlight peeked from the bottom of the hotel room curtains letting me know it was now the morning after. What happened from here? Awkwardness? Closeness? More sex?

Caleb's arm pinning me to my current position, though it was bit heavy, wasn't unpleasant. Neither was the concept of no longer being a virgin. However that, too, would take some getting used to. I felt no twinge of doubt or regret about Caleb being my first. In the very least, he knew what he was doing when it came to sex.

Perhaps my one teensy regret was blurting out that I loved him. The strong emotions I had towards him couldn't be anything but love. They were different than the indulgent and protective love I had for my little brother and more than the affection and friendship I shared with Jared.

I didn't regret loving Caleb, but with his history and personality there was a need for caution. Even if he loved me back, he was bound to get scared easily. Our relationship was already unexplored territory for him and I was afraid of making him feel tied down. At this point, his ability to commit only went so far. A slow progression into deeper feelings was needed. Caleb was emotionally a virgin. For all the sleeping around he'd done, he'd never experienced love.

Imagining him saying those three words had me thinking giddy thoughts. I loved him so much. Never had I imagined feeling this way. You couldn't truly imagine what you hadn't experienced.

Caleb tried so hard to be a good boyfriend, despite not having a romantic bone in his body. Where it really mattered, he was everything a boyfriend should be; protective, strong, caring and considerate. Therefore, I could do without the romance.

It didn't bother me that he was sort of a perv and said whatever naughty thoughts came to mind. I'd rather not be with a guy who tried to cover it up with pretty words. I wanted him to be who he really was, not what he imagined he should be for me. I loved my bad boy just the way he was.

Speaking of bad boy. . . .

I gently lifted his arm off my chest and sat up. Twisting a little and holding the sheet over my breasts, I stealthily dragged the sheet down Caleb's torso. At the point where it covered only his crotch, I stopped uncovering him.

There was a cursive word tattooed on his lower abdomen. The word "hello" was stylized in lowercase black cursive letters.

Why the hell would he have the word "hello" tattooed down there?

"Caleb!" I nudged him impatiently on the shoulder.

"Huh?" was his groggy reply.

"Wake up!"

"No." he refused, rolling over onto his stomach.

I pushed harder against his arm. "Why the do you have *hello* tattooed right above your crotch?"

That got his attention. Flipping to his side and dragging one hand over his eyes, he asked in a harassed voice, "Gianna, do we have to do this so early in the morning?"

"I want to know," I insisted stubbornly. "And it's not that early."

Raised up on one elbow now, he gave me a look, like the answer was obvious and I was too dense to grasp it. "Can't you guess?"

"No," I said, thinking hard and getting annoyed.

He sighed dramatically. "Oh, Gianna, you still think like a virgin."

I evaded his attempt to gather me in his arms. "Don't mock me, Caleb."

He stopped trying to wrap his arms around me, his expression wary. "I'm not going to apologize for who I was before I met you, Gianna."

Glaring at him for implying I'd be so stupid, I was becoming beyond annoyed. "I'm not asking you to. I just want to know what the freaking tattoo means."

"Think real hard. Who's likely to see the tattoo and in what position would she be in?"

It clicked.

My mouth dropped open in shock. "That's really bad, Caleb."

The grimace on his face and the way his body stiffened let me know he was anticipating an argument. "You know who I was before I met you."

"A freaking sex addict? How many girls have gotten on their knees to see that tattoo?"

He rubbed his jaw in a nervous gesture. "Not that many. I've only had it for six months."

I laughed humorlessly, wishing this were a nightmare. "I don't even know what to think. I mean, I know what you were like. I just didn't expect something in my face like this!" I pointed down to where the offensive tattoo was covered by the sheet once again. First time in my life I'd been offended by the word "hello."

"It's not that big of a deal, Gianna. It's just a tattoo."

"It is a big deal, Caleb, and it pisses me off that you're just blowing it off as me being the irrational girlfriend!"

"Hey, you said it. . . ."

Getting off the bed, I turned to face him. "You shouldn't have got that dumbass tattoo!"

His face hardened and he slid off the bed, grabbing his underwear from the floor to put them on in jerky movements. "Well, maybe I wouldn't have gotten it if girls didn't enjoy sucking my dick so much, moaning and panting for it."

Pain and anger sliced through me. To keep from bursting into tears, I went with the anger. "You asshole! How would you like it if I had a similar tattoo, but instead it said *Welcome All?*"

Instead of answering, Caleb grabbed a bottle of water off the nightstand and took a swig. I could have sworn his lip was twitching. If he laughed I'd throw something at him.

My misery must have seeped through my angry expression. He came around the bed, his face soft, forcing me into his arms. "I'm sorry, princess."

"I hate it," I whispered weakly, feeling a hurt I couldn't help no matter how my brain told me to be rational about it.

"I know," he responded on a squeeze.

"I may never go down on you," I warned him.

Another squeeze. "Now that's just crazy talk."

"It's not funny, Caleb. I really wish you hadn't gotten it. It's going to be a constant reminder of every girl that came before me."

He ran soothing kisses over my forehead, across my cheek. "None of them mattered. You're all that matters, Gianna."

Feeling slightly better, I laid my head against his shoulder. "That's nice to hear." Not being able to help myself, I hid a smile and said, "I'd feel a lot better about it if you changed it to say, 'hello, Gianna' instead."

His chest vibrated against me. "What would that earn me?"

Without hesitation, I answered, "Oral gratitude."

"Tempting," he teased. "How about if I just write it in with permanent marker?"

"No oral gratitude."

"I guess I'll just have to make do, then." He began tugging at the sheet wrapped about me.

I shouldn't have been surprised, but I was. "Again, Caleb? Can't I at least take a shower first?"

"No shower." With a yank, he ripped the sheet away.

Danger! Bad Boy

"You really are a sex addict!" I said in a scandalized voice, not able to hold back the grin.

"Am not!" He pretended to be offended. I imagined his next tattoo saying "Sex Addict Extraordinaire" and inwardly cringed.

He smiled wickedly. "I'm a Gianna addict."

"You better say that," I ordered sternly.

He pulled me down on to the bed. "Have mercy and feed my addiction."

He was ridiculous and exasperating, but I wouldn't change one thing about him. Except for that damn tattoo.

Like I was his own personal rag doll, Caleb situated my legs so I was on his lap straddling him. Sitting upright and satisfied with his work, he checked with one hand for my readiness while giving my nipples attention with his mouth. I circled his neck with my arms, urging him on.

I was so ready for him.

He yanked his underwear out of the way and pushed up inside of me. Leaning back some, I watched his handsome face contort in ecstasy as he groaned, closing his eyes as he slid in. As they opened to meet my avid gaze, he brushed my cheek with the back of his fingers. His smile was tender before his mouth was on mine. Did he even realize how he looked at me sometimes? His tongue stroking mine had me writhing on his lap.

With a restless sound, he gripped my hips, pumping up into me. Catching on to the rhythm he liked, I began to take over, moving up and down with him eagerly. It was *so* good. It built up to a peak and exploded throughout my body. My orgasm seemed to trigger his own. As he groaned into my breasts, a wave of warmth flowed through me. I rested my head against his. "Caleb, I love you."

His response was, "Shower time."

Still inside me, he stood up with his hands under my thighs. Carrying me into the bathroom, he set my feet down on the cool tile. I shivered as he turned away to start the shower.

He hadn't met my eyes since right before he climaxed.

The intense look on his face when he finally turned around startled me. If it was because of what I said, he could at least say what he was thinking. If he was irritated by my words, I didn't care. Well, maybe I did. But I wasn't going to hold back the emotion just because he did.

I wasn't going to pretend not to be in love with him just because he was fooling himself into believing he wasn't in love with me. Instinct told me what it was between us. It was in the way he looked at me when he wasn't convincing himself otherwise. His denial was both aggravating and oddly cute.

Our first shower together was subdued and I could only imagine the playful experience it would've been had I not freaked him out. Whatever his thoughts, he was thinking them hard. Here I was, naked and wet, and he wasn't even perving on me.

My mood wasn't helped by the fact that I was starving. How many times did a girl have to put out before she got breakfast?

Deciding to take matters into my own hands, I gave Caleb a dirty look that didn't seem to penetrate and stepped out of the shower. Screw him, his awful tattoo and his brooding. Wrapping a towel around my body, I found a pair of sweats and a tank top in his bag. Hotel room floors grossed me out, so I pulled on socks before going to the room's phone.

With the guest directory binder in my lap, I sat down on the edge of the bed. Hearing Caleb leave the bathroom, I ignored him as he sat on the bed next to me. Without looking, I sensed he was still thinking too hard. Calling room service, I handed him the binder as I waited for someone to pick up.

After ordering waffles and orange juice, I looked to Caleb. He wore only a towel around his waist. He hadn't dried off and I averted my eyes from the water droplets on his chest. I didn't want to think happy thoughts about him.

"Same," he said with an uncomfortable expression on his face. I knew it wasn't the prospect of eating waffles bothering him.

I passed along the info to the woman on the other end of the phone and got an estimate on the wait time.

Not wanting to deal with it, but not willing to go through the anxiety of avoiding the subject, I asked breezily, "What has you looking so serious?"

"Us," he answered, moving to his bag to pull out clothes. The expression I aimed for was supposed to convey bewilderment, but it faltered. Caleb sighed unhappily, coming back to sit next to me and taking one of my hands in both of his. He brushed his thumb back and forth against my knuckles.

"Gianna, I think we need to talk about what you said," he paused before adding, "Last night and this morning." His authoritative tone grated on my nerves.

"Why exactly do we need to discuss it?" This wasn't easy for me and I wasn't going to make it any easier for him.

His confidence visibly wavered as he ran a hand over his wet hair. "I care a lot about you. I just don't think we should rush into all that other stuff."

"All what other stuff?"

Caleb threw a hand in the air in agitation. "You know, all that love stuff."

"All that love stuff," I repeated tonelessly, wanting to simultaneously laugh and cry.

"Yes," he rushed to say with a hint of relief, as if I'd somehow agreed. "It ruins relationships when people get all intense like that. Then people start to form unrealistic expectations and feelings get hurt. I mean, we're having fun, right?"

"Tons," I mocked him.

He gave me a grim look. "We've been good together. We have fun. Don't you think it'd be stupid to mess with that?"

"Obviously you do," I snapped, pulling my hand out of his clasp and folding my arms over my chest defensively. "I don't want to pressure you into anything you're not ready for, Caleb."

The situation oozed with irony. I was a virgin up until last night and fearlessly transitioned into a sexual relationship with him. He was a player too terrified of love to admit to that aspect of our relationship.

I wasn't imagining it, it was there. He was just being too stubborn to face up to it.

"I don't want to hurt you, Gianna," he assured me sincerely. At least there was that. "Like I said, I care a lot about you. I don't want any other girls. I'm just not into the whole love thing."

Love stuff.

Love thing.

Who was he kidding?

A person didn't choose whether or not to love someone. Did he think I woke up one day and thought to myself, *Wouldn't it be so awesome to fall in love with my manwhore stepbrother?*

When I didn't respond, Caleb grabbed my hand again. "Gianna. . . ."

This conversation was depressing. Even if I was the girl in this relationship, I didn't want to be *the girl* in this relationship. I shuddered mentally at the thought of being whiny and clingy, always insecure and pushing for more.

No way was I begging for his love.

If he didn't want my love, then fine. Let him have it his way for now. In the end, I knew what we had was special. Everything that brought us together, every moment we'd shared told me it was love.

For a long time Caleb had been living his life with fun being his ultimate goal. The way I saw it, Caleb didn't realize a relationship based on casual fun, exclusive or not, wasn't going to make him happy. His possessiveness and the amount of time he chose to spend with me showed he was too involved for casual to work.

He was trying to backtrack to the time we first got together. Heck, even before that.

Perhaps he simply needed to be taught a lesson. He needed to learn what a relationship based solely on having fun meant.

With him eyeing me with concern, I shrugged as if it didn't matter either way. "Fine by me. I don't love you, Caleb, and you don't love me. We'll just have . . . . *fun.*"

What he needed to realize was that love didn't exclude fun. In fact, I believed it could surpass it. My agreement didn't seem to make him happy. "Why don't I like the sound of that?"

I jumped up at the knock on our door and told him over my shoulder, "You should like the sound of it, Caleb. After all, it was your idea."

CHAPTER FIVE

"You never lose by loving. You always lose by holding back."
                                                    -Barbara de Angelis

CALEB

Talk about being a sex addict.

After breakfast, I went back to sleep with Gianna, only to have her wake me up soon after by rubbing on a certain part of my anatomy.

I was a victim to her sexual whims!

With relief, I noticed our serious talk earlier hadn't seemed to phaze her. She must agree with me that getting all intense in a relationship would only ruin it in the end. I knew she'd see things my way if I explained it. Now we could just have fun together. It made for a perfect relationship.

If she hadn't seen things my way, well, I didn't know what my next step would've been.

The thought of breaking things off with her was painful.

No matter, things were settled.

All guys should have the same talk with their girlfriends. It'd result in more happy couples.

I was living the dream, having a sexfest in a Vegas hotel room with my sexy, funny, cool girlfriend.

After I made Gianna come twice, I followed her. We ended up both taking another shower before getting dressed. Since we were planning on walking up and down the strip, we dressed casually, me in jeans and a t-shirt and her in shorts and a tank top. She put on a pair of jeweled sandals her toes looked adorable peeking out of.

My god, I was turning soft. Not in my pants, never there when it came to Gianna, just in my mind. Thinking a girl's toes were cute could be a slippery slope. Next thing, I'd be painting them for her.

We walked around for a few hours, seeing the sights, letting Gianna choose where to explore. It was actually pretty boring in Vegas during the day. Unless you were gambling, all there was to do was eat or shop. I wasn't about to test our fake ids on the casino floor. Instead, we headed over to Circus Circus to play games in the arcade area.

We ate dinner at western-themed hotel restaurant then went back to our room to get ready for clubbing. Gianna looked hot in a silver skirt, black tank top and heels.

We took a taxi to the Hard Rock Hotel. There was a club there called *Body English* I'd heard good things about.

Holding Gianna's hand in the back of the taxi, occasionally stealing a kiss, it suddenly hit me that I'd never been this happy. I had the coolest, most gorgeous girlfriend in the world and we had the perfect relationship. We were totally committed to each other, without the hassle of drama caused by complex emotions.

Life was fucking fantastic.

When we got to the club, I decided there was no reason to watch how much I drank. I didn't have to drive back to the hotel or get up early tomorrow. I'd drunk the occasional beer, but hadn't been drunk in a long time. I wasn't planning on getting smashed or anything, but I was in a celebratory mood.

We danced and drank alternately for the first hour there. Then we met a group of college freshman from the University of Nevada, two girls and three guys. They seemed pretty chill and laid back, so we hung with them for the next hour or so, drinking, talking and having a good time. One of the guys, Brooks, was hilarious. I was pretty sure he was high on something, but could care less as long as he was making me laugh. If he offered any of it to Gianna, though, I'd have yanked her away from all of them.

Everything was cool until I noticed one of the other guys, Levi, leaning forward in his seat and giving Gianna flirtatious looks. At one point, the look on his face said how badly he wanted to nail her. Not about to put up with him imagining fucking my girlfriend, but unwilling to ruin the group's fun by punching him in the face, I settled for sending him killing glares until he backed down.

Satisfied I wouldn't have to kick the guy's ass, getting us thrown out of the club, I relaxed back into my seat with my arm around Gianna. Tipsy, she seemed content to lean into my side and laugh about whatever with the girl said sitting next to her.

I'd always thought the best part about going out was meeting new people. You never knew what kind of people you'd encounter. To someone drunk, just about anything was fun. With the lowered inhibitions and guard caused by drinking, you clicked with people in ways you wouldn't if you were sober. Places like this set the stage. If these people were at the same grocery store as me, we wouldn't even take notice of each other.

The third guy was Liberty and the two girls were Jana and Rita

Gianna turned to tell me she was going to the restroom with Rita. Not one minute after they took off, Jana surprised me by scooting closer to whisper in my ear the things she'd do to me back in her hotel room. I caught Levi looking at us with raised brows and a smirk. Glancing down at her, I got an eyeful of cleavage and shook my head to decline her offer.

I was shocked she'd even bother. Had she not taken a good look at the girl I was with?

Although, some of the things Jana had said, well I hoped Gianna didn't get too drunk tonight.

Jana finally moved away when we saw Gianna and Rita winding their way back through the club to us. Gianna was grinning like a madwoman when she sat back down. I had no warning before she blurted out, "Let's go to a strip club!"

Rita and Jana giggled while the guys shared a knowing look. I'd been in the middle of taking a drink of my beer and practically choked on it.

I turned to Gianna. "Why the hell would you want to do that?"

Her smile dared me to deny her. "Because I've never been to one and don't you think everyone should go to a strip club at least once in their life?"

Everyone but you, I wanted to say.

Brooks heard Gianna and shouted, "Or at least once a month!"

Suddenly, he was no longer funny.

Gianna nudged me. "Come on, Caleb. It'll be *fun*."

"Um . . . okay," I agreed reluctantly, not coming up with any good excuse to say no. For some reason, my instincts were screaming that this was a bad idea. I just couldn't put my finger on why. It was a good thing I wasn't too drunk yet. Actually, I was suddenly feeling very sober.

We took two taxis to the strip club. Gianna sat on my lap as four of us squeezed into the back of one. The strip club was only a couple blocks off the strip, taking five minutes to get there.

Something about going to a strip club with my girlfriend seemed all wrong. She wasn't acting like anything was unusual about it. Her attitude was excited and outgoing.

Once inside the club, natural male instinct had my eyes roaming to the tits and ass on display. Girlfriend or not, it was unavoidable. But my mind was on the lap dance Gianna gave me last night. Then I was remembering how good it felt to be inside her. The only place I wanted to be was back at our hotel room.

As we all sat down in much more comfortable chairs than the dance club had, a waitress strutted over to take our drink orders. Brooks tried flirting with the waitress, only to get shot down. Didn't he realize how often the servers at strip clubs got hit on?

I mostly averted my eyes from the half naked dancers wrapped around poles. Damn, some of them were athletic as hell. I didn't know if I could even do some of the gymnastic type moves they performed.

Gianna had consumed four drinks at the last club, so when she had two more in the first half hour at that strip club, I began to get worried. Her bright smile eased some of my discomfort.

Everything was fine and fucking dandy until Levi asked me and Gianna, "So, how did you guys meet?"

I choked once again on my sip of beer. Gianna giggled drunkenly before suggesting, "Why don't you take this one, Caleb?"

"Um, well," I started to say, not really knowing where to begin.

Gianna saw no reason to hesitate. "He's my stepbrother!"

They all started laughing, assuming she was joking. Noticing how unfunny I thought it was, Jana asked, "No shit? Really?"

"Really," I answered. To someone who'd just met us it might seem strange. Feeling the annoying need to explain and not wanting them to judge Gianna harshly, I added, "But my dad and her mom are getting divorced, so we won't be stepsiblings for much longer."

Rita sat up straight up in her seat. "That's so scandalous! So, was it like forbidden love and you guys couldn't help yourself?"

"How romantic!" Brooks clasped his hands together and exclaimed in a high-pitched, girly voice. How did I ever think this idiot was funny?

I shifted in my seat uncomfortably, ready to answer Rita's question, but Gianna beat me to it again. "It is so *not* love!"

Exotic dancers forgotten, Levi leaned forward. "So you two aren't serious about each other?"

"We're serious-" I began.

Gianna cut me off, swaying slightly away from me. "We're just having fun. No love involved. That makes the best relationships, don't you think?"

Levi and Liberty both looked at me in admiration. "How'd you get your girl to agree to that?"

This conversation was pissing me the hell off. Wanting off the subject, I snapped, "Love just fucks things up."

Jana and Rita both got loud in their protests. "That's such typical guy bullshit!" Jana whined.

"Total crap!" Rita agreed, then addressed Gianna directly, "You shouldn't put up with that."

Gianna tilted her head to the side thoughtfully. "I don't know. I'm kind of liking the idea. Makes things easier."

Made *what* easier? Why did her words cause me anxiety?

Jana and Rita gathered around her in some sort of girl-support cocoon that shut us guys out. "You don't have to put up with that from a guy! You're so beautiful. I bet you have guys falling at your feet, all eager to love you."

I gripped my drink tighter.

Gianna rolled her eyes, not taking them seriously. "Most of them aren't worth my time."

"And this douche is?" Rita asked, pointing at me with a thumb.

"Yeah, he isn't all that," Jana rudely chimed in. Now I felt like rolling my eyes. Little more than an hour ago she was begging me to fuck her, the two-faced slut.

These drunk bitches were pretending I wasn't sitting a yard away from them as they talked shit about me to my girlfriend. What did they know of me and Gianna? I was worried they'd infect Gianna with their stupidity. I had the sudden urge to get my girlfriend away from these people. They weren't good enough to be around her in the first place. It was like a princess hanging out in a whorehouse.

"Oh shit, you're in trouble," Liberty joked. When the quiet person in the group spoke up, it was a sign the situation was escalating.

Gianna waved her hand in the air nonchalantly. "Don't worry about it, I'm not."

With incredibly bad timing, one of the strippers came by asking, "Does anyone want a lap dance?"

Gianna perked up, holding her hand out to me. "I need some cash."

"What the hell for?" I asked in alarm, not liking the calculating look in her eyes.

"Just give me the money, Caleb," she ordered in an exasperated tone.

I took out my wallet and handed her some twenties. Snatching them out of my hand, she leaned over to kiss my cheek. "Thanks, babe."

She gave them to the stripper saying, "My boyfriend needs a lap dance."

"Gianna, what the fuck are you doing?" I exploded. If I wanted a lap dance, I'd get it from my girlfriend. That was what the fuck she was for.

She looked at me angelically. "Sheesh, lighten up, Caleb. Learn to have some *fun*."

Brooks laughed obnoxiously, making me want to break his nose. Levi thumped my shoulder in encouragement. Liberty appeared to be the only one wary of a girlfriend getting her boyfriend a lap dance.

Brooks shouted, "That's how every girlfriend should treat her man!"

What, by making him pay for a lap dance he didn't fucking want in the first place?

Rita and Jana looked disgusted and annoyed. Stupid drunk bitches.

I was angry with Gianna for making a spectacle of our relationship. Surprisingly, I was also slightly hurt she'd treat what we had like it was nothing. It occurred to me that perhaps she was acting out just to mess with me. Was she trying to teach me a lesson?

The suspicion was growing stronger. If so, two could play at that game.

It was time to start the show. I slouched back in my chair and patted my lap for the stripper. I discreetly watched Gianna's eyes narrow. I turned my head to full on look at her and saw her paste an unconcerned smile on her face.

The stripper swayed over seductively with a wicked smile on her face. I had to admit she was hot. Nice body, fake boobs, lots of platinum hair, pretty enough face. Normally I'd be pleased by the attention, enjoy the sexually charged moment. Having a girlfriend I was committed to changed everything. Even if my girlfriend was acting like a brat in need of a spanking.

However, Gianna started this game and I planned on winning it. Teach her a lesson of her own. I sat there seemingly willing while the stripper grinded on my lap. During most of the dance, I stared into Gianna's eyes.

The stripper wore nothing but a thong, making my dick get hard with the combination of that and her movements. It didn't help I was having flashbacks of Gianna doing some of the same moves on my lap the night before.

The stripper rubbed her boobs against my chest and whispered in my ear, "You're cuter than my usual customers."

I didn't comment back. Maybe the stripper was into me or maybe she made every guy she straddled believe he was that rare customer who actually turned her on in return. This situation was fucked up. I wasn't supposed to be in a Vegas strip club with my girlfriend looking on while a stripper ground her pussy into my dick.

Moving my gaze from the tits in my face to the hurt in Gianna's eyes she was trying to hide with a phony smile had me ready to admit defeat. Maybe winning wasn't worth it. Whatever the hell game she was playing, it was causing her pain. The last thing I ever wanted to do was hurt her. The thought drove me crazy.

The stripper finished off her performance, whispering in my ear again, "I'm off in an hour."

Yeah, how much would that cost me?

Guys like Levi or Brooks would've taken her up on that. The old me would've had her in my hotel room in an hour and a half, making Dante find somewhere else to be.

But that was the old me.

The stripper was in her early twenties and she wouldn't have been the first female I let think I was older than my sixteen years. Not that I hadn't fucked older girls with them knowing full well I was underage.

Abruptly, the thought of older guys fucking Gianna popped into my head, making me see red. Which was ridiculous since I was the only guy in Gianna's short sexual history. As much fun as I'd had getting laid in the past, the thought of Gianna acting the same way disgusted me. Whether it made me an asshole or not, I couldn't help feeling that way.

The stripper sauntered off, on the prowl for her next easy money. Lost in a mass of conflicting thoughts, I stared off after her.

Levi got my attention by saying, "Hey, man, when you're done having fun with Gianna, can I have a little fun of my own?"

I pushed his shoulder to get him away from me. Incredibly pissed off, I couldn't shake the feeling of doom. I was playing a game with Gianna tonight I didn't fully understand. Had I made the wrong decision with the stripper? In retrospect, Gianna could have been testing me in a way I'd just failed.

Gianna got up, announcing she was going to the restroom with Rita. Before I realized what was about to happen, Levi grabbed her around the waist to pull her down on his lap. "My turn. How about giving me a lap dance, Gianna?"

Gianna hands went up, maybe to wrap her arms around his neck, maybe to push him away.

I didn't wait to see. Standing up, I yanked her off his lap, giving him a killing look and debating whether or not to start a fight in a strip club. I definitely didn't want to be dragged out of here by the gargantuan bouncers.

Looking unhappy, Gianna laughed humorlessly. "What's the matter, Caleb? We're only having fun. It's not like we're in love."

So that was her game.

I retained my grip on her arm and told the stupid fuckers we'd met tonight, "We're leaving." No reason to exchange numbers, except for maybe Liberty they were all dumb shits.

Our new friends looked a little alarmed, but didn't make a move to interfere. That solidified it. I knew I'd never physically hurt Gianna, but they didn't know me well enough to make that call.

Maybe there were instances when meeting new people was a waste of time.

Gianna called out, "It was nice meeting you guys!"

Stepping out into the warm Vegas night, she turned to me. "I thought we were having fun?"

CHAPTER SIX

"True love cannot be found where it does not truly exist;
nor can it be hidden where it does."
-David Schwimmer

CALEB

Tonight was not going as planned. Gianna had managed to throw all my words in my face. My idea of a committed relationship with no love involved hadn't turned out as planned either.

We were driving back to the hotel sitting on opposite sides of the backseat in our taxi. Gianna had her eyes closed and was leaning her head against the window. I stared at her for a whole minute as she ignored my presence.

"Quit pretending to sleep, Gianna."

"Caleb," she paused, "It's in both of our best interests that I'm pretending to sleep."

"What the hell is that supposed to mean?" I asked in aggravation.

Her eyes remained closed. "I don't want to be the drunk, crazy girlfriend. I think I've made enough of a fool of myself during this trip."

I grabbed her arm and dragged her towards me. "Come here, princess."

She tried to pull away. "Just leave it alone, Caleb."

"Leave what alone? I still don't understand what the hell is going on!"

I noticed the cabbie looking at us in his rearview mirror. When she didn't respond, I let it go for now. Minutes later, we were dropped off in front of our hotel and I handed the driver money before rushing in after Gianna.

We traveled in silence through the hazy hotel casino, up the elevator and into our hotel room. As I shut the door, flipping the latch, Gianna escaped into the bathroom. After ten minutes she hadn't come out and I couldn't hear the shower running.

Moving over to the closed door, I put my ear against it.

Fuck!

She was crying.

Restless, I knocked on the door. "Baby, open the door."

She didn't answer, but I heard the faucet turn on.

I said calmly, but in a tone that let her know how serious I was, "Gianna, I will break this door down. I really don't want to have to pay for it, but I will."

She opened the door a minute later with her face freshly washed. Leaning against the doorframe, she asked quietly, "What?"

"Why were you crying?" My tone was harsher than intended, but I didn't like what I was feeling. Everything that happened tonight was crap, fucked up and unnecessary.

She stared down the floor. "I wasn't crying."

"I heard you," I managed to say in a softer voice. I wanted to reach out and hold her, but something about her posture told me she'd prefer I didn't.

"I'm tired. I'm going to go to sleep." She circled around me, bending over her bag to pull out something to sleep in. Past girlfriend experience would've probably helped me in this situation. Unfortunately, I was flying blind here.

Coming up behind her, I wrapped my arms around her waist and pulled her back onto my lap as I sat on the bed. Burying my face in her neck, I took in all that was her, needing to make things right between us again. "Please tell me what's wrong, princess. You're killing me."

"It's no use." She shrugged her shoulders in a jerky movement.

"What's no use?"

She turned sideways on my lap to look me in the eyes. "Let's just fuck, Caleb."

Her words were jarring. The way she said them making it seem crude. I ignored her obvious ploy to distract me. "No."

Her face was pure disbelief as her dark blonde eyebrows rose. "No?"

Raising my thumb, I stroked her silky cheek. Her flinch was far from reassuring. Tightening my arm around her, I had the urge to somehow chain her to me so nothing could ever tear her away from me. "Baby, please talk to me."

Her eyes welled up with tears. It hurt to watch.

She sniffled and said in a hoarse voice. "You had a hard on."

I had to choke back my laughter. She must have felt my chest shake because her eyes narrowed. "Gianna, if you don't want me to get a hard on for other girls, then don't throw naked strippers onto my lap."

Her bottom lip pouted adorably. "Did you want her?"

"No," I returned without hesitation.

"But you had a hard on for her!" she protested.

I shook my head, wishing we weren't having this conversation. "Gianna, guys can't help things like that. Did I have a hard on? Yes. Did I want to use it on her? Not one bit."

"Oh," she said in confusion, obviously not in complete understanding. She met my eyes again and asked with hope in her voice, "So, what you're saying is that it was involuntary?"

"Exactly."

She stared at me for so long I began wondering what she was thinking. Her expression brightened somewhat and she almost smiled. "Okay, Caleb, I forgive you for that."

Was there something else I needed to be forgiven for?

"I need a drink," I muttered to myself and set her on the bed so I could walk over to the mini fridge where I'd stored the alcohol we didn't drink last night. Pulling out a cold beer, I contemplated a wine cooler for her, but left it, deciding Gianna was more than drunk enough already.

When I turned back around, she sat on the bed with a playful look on her face. "I like you, Caleb."

Uncontrollably, I scowled at her. Something about that sounded wrong.

Her smile grew. "I liked Levi, too. He was cool."

Oh, hell no.

Pointing at her I said, "Don't think you're out of trouble when it comes to him."

Wearing a slightly astonished expression on her beautiful face, she said, "What are you talking about? I thought he was fun."

Giving her an unhappy look, I chugged the last of my beer and slammed it down on the dresser. Pulling off my shirt, I told her, "Take off your clothes."

Smiling, she slowly began to undress. I was naked by the time she had her skirt and top off. Hooking two fingers into the waistband of her panties, I pulled her towards me. She squealed in surprise, but when I checked between her legs, she was wet for me.

I practically ripped off her panties and bra in my attempt to get at the good stuff. I jammed two fingers in her and took one nipple into my mouth. Biting down lightly, I savored her whimper and her arousal.

Fingering her, I brought my head up to say in her ear, "I better not ever see you let a guy touch you like that again."

"He only pulled me onto his lap," she responded breathlessly.

"You're mine, Gianna. No one touches you but me." I kissed her possessively while driving my fingers deep to drive the point home. She came around my fingers, moaning her pleasure against my lips. Pulling my fingers out, I got in position and thrusted between her splayed legs.

"We were only having fun," Gianna gasped.

Pressing my forehead against hers, I demanded, "Say you're mine, Gianna."

With her hands in my hair, she kissed me, stroking my tongue with hers sweetly. "I'm yours Caleb . . . for as long as we like each other."

Finding heaven being with her like this, I didn't care about anything but that moment. "You love me, Gianna."

She closed her eyes, shaking her head. "I'm not allowed to."

Moving faster, wanting to make her as mindless as me, I rubbed her clit with my thumb. "Say it, Gianna."

"No, you don't love me back." Gripping my shoulders, she was close to another climax. "Caleb!"

"Say it, baby. Let me hear it on your sweet lips as I fuck you."

Her hair wild on the pillow, her face showing her pleasure, she came. "I love you, Caleb!"

Her pussy tightened its grip on me. I shut my eyes at the sensation, opening them to see her eyes half-closed as gazed up at me. "That's my girl."

After coming, I fell forward, elbows on either side of her to keep from crushing her. Moving my lips from one flushed cheek to the other, I smoothed her hair back from her forehead. "Don't worry. I won't ever want anyone else. It's you and me forever, Gianna."

She wrapped shaky arms around my neck, turning her face into my neck. "I love you, Caleb. I know you love me, too."

"Go to sleep, princess." Dropping to her left side, I dragged the blanket over us. With her head on my chest, she went to sleep.

Running fingers lightly up and down her back, feeling a deep sense of peace, I dozed off.

Asleep only a couple hours, I woke up needing to use the restroom. I decided to take a quick shower. Under the spray, I thought back on our crazy night. It started rough but had ended spectacularly.

Walking out of the bathroom, I ran my eyes over the sexy girl in bed. Going over to the dresser, I grabbed my phone. It was past one in the morning and I'd had the ringer off all night. Dante had left a message just after midnight that I quickly returned. I ignored the messages from chicks. That was a message in itself.

There was a text message from Julie that said, "You need to call me ASAP!"

Uptight bitch.

My first instinct was to ignore it, but I decided it was better to know what she was up to. Not wanting to wake up Gianna, I pulled on some jeans, grabbed a room key and stepped into the hallway.

I called Julie, wondering if she'd even answer this late. She did so on the third ring.

Without saying hello, she immediately snapped in a hate-filled tone, "You need to bring my daughter home."

Like I hadn't been expecting that one.

"I'll have to disagree."

"Are you fucking her?" she asked angrily. What happened to the 50s housewife throwback? Her potty mouth was going to ruin the perfect image she tried so hard to project.

"That's none of your business," I told her, not able to help myself from adding, "And very crude, Julie."

"I swear, if you get her pregnant. . . ." she trailed off, probably imagining a screaming miniature version of me. It'd be a damn handsome baby boy.

"If I got her pregnant, you'd be the youngest grandma in the neighborhood," I taunted her. Still only thirty-three, Julie was already young to be the mother of a sixteen-year-old.

"I've already talked to her father about her running away. When she returns, I'm sending her to live with him in Houston," she informed me smugly.

Her words jolted me out of my cocky attitude. "You can't do that!" I practically shouted in my panic.

"I can do whatever I want. She's a minor and I'm her mother."

"But she'll have to leave her entire life behind." I almost blurted out she'd have to leave me behind. I couldn't lose her and what we had. I'd never been so freaking happy in my life. Plus, she's hate leaving Denver and her crew. Before I came along they were her life, everything that was important to her.

"Bring her back tomorrow and I'll let her stay in Denver," Julie offered, probably reluctant of giving Gianna up to Houston herself. It'd be hard to control Gianna from so far away.

"And you'll leave us alone?" I asked cautiously.

"No, that's not part of the deal. You bring her back and break up with her, or I'll ship her off to Houston and far away from your influence."

"You're a real bitch, Julie."

"No, I'm a mother who wants the best for her daughter. I have plans for her life which don't include her ending up with some loser delinquent."

I banged my head against the wall. "I hate you."

Sounding uncaring, she said, "Either way it's your choice, Caleb. You have until tomorrow night to get my daughter home and end it with her, or I ship her off to her father."

I hung up on her venom and would've punched the wall, but I knew the hotel had cameras in the hallways. My hand trembling, I slipped the key card through the slot to let me back into the room.

Too hyped up and upset to go back to sleep, I stood at the end of the bed staring down at Gianna. She was curled up in sleep, blissfully unaware of her mom's latest threats. If I told Julie to shove it, she'd send Gianna to Houston. I could always try talking my parents into letting me follow her, but what if Julie sent her somewhere else where I couldn't get to her?

If she got Gianna's dad and his money on her side, they could decide to send her to boarding school in England, or some crazy shit like that. In addition to leaving me, she'd be ripped away from the friends who were so important to her. I didn't know how she'd handle losing that support system if she lost them.

I pictured some preppy British fuck hitting on her with his pretentious accent and ran a hand over my face to keep from losing my shit. Not that some cowboy with a Texan accent doing it would be any better.

At least in Denver she'd still be near. I'd be able to watch her from afar. Christ, that sounded lame. If I broke up with her, then I'd lose her and she'd lose me, but she'd still have her friends. In Houston she'd be starting completely over.

The selfish thing to do would be to call Julie's bluff, try to hold on to her. But at what cost to Gianna? She'd possibly lose everything and we'd be separated anyway.

The unselfish thing would be to let her go. She'd lose nothing except what we had.

In this moment, I knew without a doubt that I loved her because I could feel my heart being ripped apart in my chest.

CHAPTER SEVEN

"You know it's love when all you want is that person to be happy, even if you're not part of their happiness."
-Julia Roberts

GIANNA

I woke up in our Las Vegas hotel to a slight headache and a serious looking Caleb. He was propped up on his elbow in bed next to me, staring down at me.

The boy wouldn't admit he loved me, but he watched me sleep? If that didn't scream *I love you* then I didn't know what did. Okay, well maybe the actual words would be more effective.

He'd come around. I had all the time in the world to wait for him to vocalize his feelings.

I gazed at him silently in return, adding a small smile. Then I noticed the bags under his eyes and the weariness on his face. Reaching up, I touched his cheek. He hadn't shaved since yesterday morning and his stubble was rough under my hand. I liked it.

"What's the matter, Caleb? Didn't you sleep?"

"I couldn't." The defeated look in his eyes was weird. We'd made up last night, so it couldn't be that.

I tried to lighten his mood. "Well, I slept like a baby. You wore me out, stud."

It didn't work. Still silent, he leaned down and surprised me with how passionately he kissed me. My eyes went wide in shock, only to see an uncharacteristic intensity in his. I wrapped my arms behind his neck and welcomed the unexpected intimacy.

I loved him so much. I was lost in the feel of his hands roaming my body. Touching more than just the outside, I felt like he was stroking the inside of me as well, my heart and soul.

For the first time, Caleb made love to me.

His face turned away from me, I was sure he'd gotten tears in his eyes, too.

Afterwards, holding me in his arms, his face pressed into my neck, I basked in the afterglow. I tried moving my head to the side to look at him, but he jumped up off the bed and disappeared into bathroom, still not saying a word.

Okay. What the hell was going on with him?

He came out fifteen minutes later, showered and changed. I laid there in bed, feeling unsure about what was going on in his head, when he finally said, "Get ready. We're going home."

With that, he grabbed the room key off the nightstand and left the hotel room.

Okay. What *the hell* was going on?

CALEB

I had to get away from her. Even looking at her was painful. Each of her smiles clawed at my heart. I tried telling myself we were going home because it was time, but I knew the truth. I was being forced to let her go.

Unless I could think of some way to hold onto her it would be the end of us. I needed a plan that didn't involving poisoning her mother. Prison would separate us more permanently. I loved Gianna so fucking much that the feeling of being apart from her for any period of time had me panicking.

I sat down with a bottle of water in an armchair in the hotel lobby, obsessing over the situation. An idea came to me. Julie could just *think* we'd broken up. We'd snuck around behind Julie's back before. She'd been completely ignorant before Josh opened his big trap. Now we'd simply have to be even sneakier. I tossed the empty bottle into a trashcan and rushed back up to the hotel room, feeling much better about the situation.

GIANNA

Hair wet from a shower, I was pulling a shirt over my head when Caleb came back in a much better mood. He pounced on me, dragging me into his arms and swinging me around.

"Did someone just take their antidepressants?" I teased him.

He threw his head back and laughed. "Something like that."

His kiss was infused with happiness. I welcomed it as much as the passionate, intense kisses from earlier. Gathering our things, we took the elevator down to check out. I sensed our Vegas trip had brought us closer, but I wouldn't miss the smoky smell in all the casinos.

Thirty minutes later, we were on the highway out of Sin City. We stopped an hour or so outside of Vegas in Mesquite, Nevada to eat a late breakfast at a diner. Caleb explained he was eager to get home so he wanted to drive the whole way today, getting us home sometime tonight.

We kept our stops to a minimum in order to make good time. A few hours outside of Denver, just over the Colorado border, it was early evening when we stopped at a fast food restaurant to use the restroom and grab some food. I told Caleb what I wanted to eat and went to the women's restroom while he ordered for us.

When I came out, his mood had changed again.

CALEB

Three hours away from Denver, we stopped at a fast food restaurant to eat. While Gianna was using the restroom, I got a text message from Julie.

Julie: *Don't think to trick me, Caleb. I know your kind. My daughter better be on her way home. Call me.*

I could tell Gianna was confused by my sour mood, but how did I explain? I'd been planning on breaking it all down to her before we reached home. I'd been sure she'd agree sneaking around was the best plan in dealing with Julie. In less than two years we'd been eighteen and could tell her mom to go fuck herself. Besides, I'd have thought of something else before then.

Now, I wasn't so sure.

When Gianna started eating her chicken strips, I went outside to make the call. My appetite was gone. Julie answered on the second ring. "Where are you?"

"Hello to you, too, mommy dearest," I said sarcastically.

"Not for long." The distaste was evident in her voice.

I didn't want to be infected with her poison. The crap she was putting us all through, Gianna, me and my dad, was unbelievable. Not to mention what Gianna's little brother was experiencing being alone in that house with her. All for her screwed up vision of the perfect life she wanted for her daughter.

"We're three hours away."

"What have you told her?" she asked suspiciously.

"Nothing yet," I snapped at her.

"Keep it that way for now," she paused, "And don't think to try and fool me, Caleb. You won't be able to deceive me. Trying to sneak behind my back to see her won't work. Trust me, I'll use whoever I have to in order to find out. Her friends, the administration at the school, the mailman, a private detective. Whatever it takes."

"Okay psycho, you don't have to convince me."

There went that plan.

She ignored my name calling and continued, "When you arrive at the house, come inside with her. Follow my lead and don't deny anything I say."

"What are you planning?" I asked warily. Crazy ass bitch was capable of anything.

She sounded smug as she said vaguely, "Just making sure there are no loose ends." Her voice turned hard with her next words, "Don't doubt I'm sincere, Caleb. I'll send Gianna away from her family in order to secure her future. A future that does *not* include a loser delinquent like you."

"Fuck you, Julie!"

"No more than four hours, Caleb. I'll be expecting you both."

She hung up before I could get out the rest of what I had to say to her.

GIANNA

Eating my food, I could see Caleb through the large restaurant windows, standing in the parking lot and talking on his cell phone. He appeared to be arguing with someone. I figured it was his mom or dad. They had to be pissed we'd taken off like that. I watched as he ended the call, looking like he wanted to throw his phone across the parking lot. He stalked back inside but didn't touch his food.

"Aren't you hungry?" I pointed to his hamburger and fries.

His only answer was to start eating. I finished the last of my fries and stood up with my trash. He didn't utter a peep as I walked out of the restaurant. I wasn't sure he even looked up from his meal. Leaning against his car, I waited for him to join me.

He exited the place a minute later, unlocking my side first then walking around the car to get behind the wheel. Once we were back on the highway, I exploded. "What the hell is your problem, Caleb?"

"I don't have a problem," he responded calmly, but I could his see his knuckles turn white from his death grip on the steering wheel.

"If you say so," I said sarcastically. Turning up the stereo, I watched the scenery out the window for the next hour. Western Colorado desert transformed into lush green mountain scenery. While passing over the Rockies, I must've fallen asleep because I woke up to him nudging me in the shoulder.

"We're almost there," he explained in a tense voice.

I blinked open my eyes to see the lights of the city in the distance come into focus.

Back in Denver.

Back to reality.

We were on the I-70 descent down the mountain and into the outlying suburbs.

Thirty short minutes later we were on the freeway and exiting into Broomfield. I felt extremely nervous about facing my mom. But with Caleb by my side, I'd find the strength. My mom would never be able to tear us apart. I loved Caleb and even though he hadn't said the words aloud, I knew he loved me, too.

Glancing over at Caleb, I saw he was still in a bad mood. He was probably just worried or stressed about dealing with my mom. It sucked to be the one with the crazy parent. His dad, Scott, was so cool about us, even though it was breaking up his marriage. Hopefully he'd be happier away from my mom, like *my* dad was.

CALEB

The closer we got to Gianna's house, the tighter my chest felt. I had to think of something.

Fast.

Nothing came to me. It didn't help that I was spazzing out inside. I didn't doubt Julie's words. She was crazy enough to send her daughter to Siberia to get her away from me. As adorable as Gianna would be all bundled up like an Eskimo, I didn't relish the thought of seeing it on Skype.

I glanced over at Gianna and although she seemed agitated, she managed to give me a quick smile. Maybe we could just keep driving through Denver, all the way to the East coast. If we weren't so young, it might've worked. Unfortunately, two sixteen-year-olds on their own wouldn't fare well. A psychotic mother looking for them would only hurt their chances. I could just imagine Julie's heartfelt pleas to the media, desperate to find her missing daughter. She'd probably find a way to get me thrown me into prison

I didn't want all that insanity for Gianna.

Plus, my money would only last so long, only go so far. What would we do after that? Get jobs at McDonald's? Maybe Julie was right and Gianna did deserve better than me.

Still without any alternative or a plan, I pulled my car into the driveway of Gianna's house, turning off the engine reluctantly. Grabbing her suitcase out of the trunk, I followed her to the front door then inside the house.

Where Julie was waiting.

For the past couple days I'd experienced heaven and now I was entering hell.

GIANNA

I shouldn't have been surprised to see my mom standing in the entryway of the house when we walked in, but I was. Had she been looking out the window when we pulled up in Caleb's car?

Her arms were crossed over her chest and she had a calculating look on her face. She ignored me and looked to Caleb. "So, you're finished with her?"

What the hell? She'd really gone insane this time. "Mom, what are you talking about?"

I glanced at Caleb but he didn't seem to be experiencing my confusion. His expression was blank, closed off. He didn't respond to my mom's crazy question.

I started to get a bad feeling in the pit of my stomach and an ache in my chest.

My mom continued, this time addressing me, a softer expression on her face, "Gianna, I tried to protect you from guys like him."

I shook my head, wanting out of this confrontation. "What are you talking about? What on earth could I need protecting from?"

My mom gave Caleb a pointed look and he finally said, "Me."

I laughed, this was ridiculous. "You two are going to have to explain this to me. I don't quite understand. Why would you be worried about Caleb hurting me?"

My mom had a resigned look on her face. "I really wish you hadn't taken off with him like that, Gianna. If you'd only given me a chance to warn you." She shook her head in sorrow. "As your mother, I only blame myself."

I knew underneath all the crazy my mom loved me. She just had so many issues from when she was a teenager and the way my dad divorced her. She needed to let it go and let me live my life the way I wanted.

I moved closer to Caleb. "There's nothing to warn me about. I think I know Caleb a little better than you do."

"No, you don't," she disagreed solemnly.

"Just spit it out, Julie," Caleb muttered with a thread of menace in his voice and the coldest look I'd ever seen on his face.

She glanced at him sharply. "Caleb is on probation, Gianna."

"Yeah, I know."

"You do?" Caleb looked at me in surprise before nodding his head, "Oh yeah, Ian opened his big mouth."

My mom was also surprised at my knowledge. Her eyes narrowed. "Do you know what for?"

I crossed my arms, not caring. "No, and it doesn't matter."

"He almost beat a guy to death." she rasped harshly.

I flinched, my turn to be shocked. The thought had never crossed my mind it could be for a violent crime. I'd assumed it would be for possession or something like that.

"It doesn't matter," I ground out through clenched teeth. The determination in my voice had faltered a bit. I stared at Caleb, knowing I had nothing to fear from him. But I was thrown off when he didn't meet my gaze.

My mom shifted, bringing my attention back to her. She seemed more determined than before. "He's a gigolo."

CALEB

I couldn't believe Julie just went there. It wasn't entirely accurate, but not completely false either. I opened my mouth to defend myself, but then closed it, thinking of Julie's threats. I had no choice but to go along with whatever the bitch said. I had no idea how she even knew of Claudette.

My dad must have told her. Big fucking mistake on his part, to ever trust a woman like Julie.

As much as it hurt to let this happen, maybe all of these *revelations* about me would help ease Gianna's pain in the end. Help her to get over me. I'd be willing to take on more pain to lessen the amount she felt.

Gianna's mouth was hanging open in shock. "Mom, that's insane. Besides, what the hell do you mean by gigolo? Is that the old school term for player?"

Julie gave Gianna a serious look, but I could see the triumphant gleam in her eyes. "It means he had a sexual relationship with an older woman and in return, she took care of him. Buying him things, giving him money."

Gianna's shock turned to understanding as she looked at me with wide blue eyes. "That's where all the money came from."

I didn't deny it. It was mostly the truth. My parents gave me an allowance, but it was small compared to the rest of my money.

Despite all of that, Gianna moved even closer to me, reaching out to wrap her arms around my waist from the side. "I don't care about that, either. It's in his past." Her voice trembled on her next words, "I love him, mom."

I couldn't allow myself to hold her in return.

Looking down at the top of her head, loving her all the more for her understanding, it killed me. It was killing me that she loved me despite my past and I couldn't let her know how much it meant to me.

Julie scowled, but I suspected she wasn't ready to admit defeat. Of course she wasn't.

She stepped closer to us. "You may love him, Gianna, but he doesn't love you."

Fucking evil cunt! I hated her more than ever.

"He does," Gianna whispered then tilted her head up at me. She looked so sure. She had reason to be. Everything I'd ever done for her had proven the love I hadn't been able to admit to.

"Ask him," Julie demanded.

Gianna blushed, embarrassed by the fucked up situation we'd found ourselves in. "Tell her she's wrong, Caleb."

This was where it ended. If I told her I loved her, Julie would lose this battle but win the war by sending Gianna to Houston. If I denied loving Gianna, we'd be over but Gianna could at least return to the life she had before me.

Staring into her eyes, I told Gianna in a steady voice, "I can't."

Gianna's smile faltered and I sensed Julie struggling to contain her glee. "Of course you can," Gianna assured me.

I would have loved to. I couldn't. There was no other choice.

Everything in my past seemed so trivial, unimportant compared to what was happening at this very moment. I braced myself for the biggest lie of my life.

Looking straight into her confused eyes, I attempted to control my chaotic emotions. "I don't love you, Gianna."

She flinched, her arms dropping to her sides, and backed away from me. "Maybe it's too soon, but you're falling in love with me." Her voice turned hopeful by the end of the sentence.

I shook my head as if I pitied her. I pitied us both. "I'm not. I won't."

On the verge of tears, she asked, "After everything we've been through?"

"No."

She broke eye contact to stare down at the floor. Her entire body stiffened, like she was holding herself in check. I shot Julie a look of pure hatred that passed right over her. Her eyes were glowing in triumph. Gianna's head was still bowed as her mom's expression turned hard, letting me know she wouldn't back down.

Still looking at the floor, Gianna asked, "Do you really even want to be with me?"

Clearing my throat, I took my time answering, hating the lie I was about to utter. "Not anymore. We had fun, but I think it has run its course."

I expected her to start crying at any moment, but when she looked back up at me, she wasn't crying. I thought she'd rage at me. According to my callous words, I deserved it.

Danger! Bad Boy

She didn't know I would tear out my heart to make hers stop bleeding.

Gianna's voice was emotionless, her face expressionless, as she finally said, "I don't want to ever see you again, Caleb."

With that parting shot, she dashed past her mom and up the stairs.

CHAPTER EIGHT

"The greater your capacity to love, the greater your capacity to feel the pain."
-Jennifer Aniston

GIANNA

Climbing up the stairs, once out of sight, I ran to my room. Slamming the door shut, I belatedly worried about waking up Chance. My chest felt like it was about to explode.

I couldn't breathe.

Was this what hyperventilating was?

I still wasn't crying. Shouldn't I be crying? Didn't people cry when they had a broken heart?

Maybe it was shock. That was it, I was in shock.

What just happened? Did that just happen? Maybe I was still at the hotel in Las Vegas.

Asleep.

Dreaming.

Oh god! *Please let this have been a nightmare.*

I heard yelling downstairs. I cracked open my door to listen to my mom yelling at Caleb to leave the house.

Please don't leave.

Seconds later, the front door slammed shut. I rushed to my bedroom window to look down at the driveway below.

Caleb got into his car.

Please come back.

Please tell me you love me.

Please tell me it was all a lie.

His car started. I held my breath.

The red Camaro pulled out of the driveway. I gripped the windowsill tightly.

The pain told me I wasn't dreaming. This wasn't an awful nightmare.

He drove down the street, stopping at the stop sign before turning around the corner and out of sight.

My body started shaking with the emotions I was now trying to hold back. It was getting even harder to breathe. I turned away from the window, away from the sight of the empty street.

I looked frantically around my room. Something had to fix this. How did I fix this? How did I stop feeling this horrible pain?

I caught sight of my antique 1980s boombox on my dresser. One of my prized possessions.

As I threw it through my bedroom window, glass shattering, the tight hold I had on my emotions shattered too.

Bastard!

I dropped to the floor, sobbing.

CALEB

Driving from Gianna's house to my dad's old condo a suburb away in Northglenn, I was doing what I'd thought was impossible.

Crying over a girl.

Shit.

Had all that just happened?

Could I have handled it any differently? If only Julie hadn't given me a deadline to get her home. I had no doubt the crazy bitch would've had her on the next plane to Houston had I not gotten Gianna home by tonight.

If only I'd had more time. Even now, I couldn't think of any way out of Julie's ultimatum. I'd had no other choice. If I hadn't broken up with Gianna, then she would've sent her away. If I'd followed Gianna to Houston, she would have sent her further away until she was out of my reach.

Gianna wouldn't turn eighteen for almost two years. Julie could act like a tyrant until then.

Maybe I should've told Gianna. No, that would've been a mistake. She wouldn't have accepted what must be done. She would have tried to hold on to our relationship and fight her mom. Her mom was determined as hell.

Her mom would've won and Gianna would've been on the next plane to Houston. Gianna's entire life would change as she was forced to start over. I just hoped those friends, the crew that were so important to her, were there for her through this.

She loved me just as much as I loved her, I had no doubt. This wouldn't be easy on her. In fact, it'd probably be harder. At least I knew she loved me. For her, I was just an asshole who used her for a good time.

That douche Jared would be happy to hear about what happened.

The lie Julie forced me to spit out was eating me up inside. For Gianna to think I didn't love her made me sick.

Not as bad, but still bad, were the things Julie told her about my past. About the guy I put in the hospital.

About Claudette.

I tried not to think about that part of my past. I'd definitely never wanted Gianna to find out about it. Now I wasn't only the asshole who used her, I was the scumbag who used her.

Fuck.

Gianna.

She mostly likely despised me now. I knew she had to. She told me she never wanted to see me again.

With the way things just ended, I didn't blame her.

I'd never regret one second of being with her, though. She was my first love. My only love. My true love. With or without her, she was my everything.

When she turned eighteen, nothing would stop me from winning her back.

Of all the horrible things I'd done to chicks, this was the worst. Whether it was my fault or not, whether I had a choice or not, I'd hurt her badly.

GIANNA

After what seemed like hours of crying and ignoring my mom's knocking on the door, I literally picked myself up off the floor.

Everyone had been right.

Caleb was and always would be a player.

He didn't love me, told me he never would.

He took my virginity and my love so easily only to throw me away. I trusted him too much. I gave him too much of me. Told him things I'd never told anyone else and opened myself up to him.

This had been a lesson well learned.

He'd see that he hadn't broken me. He would never get to see my pain, my tears, my heartbreak.

Everything had been a mistake from the moment I'd met him. *Everything.*

Mistakes could be fixed.

He'd never know how much he hurt me. I'd played a role before, I could do it again.

CALEB

Friday morning, I didn't know if Gianna would show up to school after what happened the night before. I wasn't really up to going myself after not sleeping all night, but I had to be there just in case she was.

I dragged myself out of a bed that I saw no sleep in. Thirty minutes later, I was back in Broomfield, pulling my car into the school parking lot. As I looked for a parking space, I scanned the cars I passed, looking for Gianna's Jeep.

She probably wouldn't come. Girls took these things hard. Not that I was taking it any better. I just needed to see her. I needed to see that she was okay.

After parking, I stepped out of my car and leaned against the trunk, waiting for her to show up. If she did at all.

Three minutes before the first bell rang, I was about to give up. Concentrating on the entrances to the parking lot, it barely registered with me when that Seth guy drove by me and waved with a smile on his face.

Were we friends? I didn't think so. After one date with Gianna, I'd kind of snatched her right out from under him. Right out from under Jared, too. Both guys had reason to not be friendly towards me. Not that I gave a fuck.

I was still looking at the entrance of the parking lot when I heard a girl squeal, "Gianna!" I turned my head swiftly toward the sound. A group of cheerleaders were skipping across the parking lot like a herd of gazelles. My gaze followed the direction they were heading.

And I saw her.

Getting out of the passenger side of Seth's car.

Wearing her cheerleader uniform once again.

Fake smile plastered on her face.

The old Gianna was back.

GIANNA

And I'd thought school was torture before I met Caleb.

Now it was excruciating.

I ignored Caleb's presence the best I could during the two classes we shared before lunch. But now that it was lunch the questions came. I was sitting with my old *friends,* the jocks and cheerleaders, all of them eager to have the queen of popularity back on her throne.

I felt like pulling out my hair. I felt like pulling a Britney Spears and shaving it all off. See how much they'd want me then.

At the same time, there was comfort and a sense of security in once again being surrounded by all the phoniness. I'd rather endure their deceptions than ever experience Caleb's again. I could hide from him amongst them. Hide from reality and the pain.

I realized he'd never said he loved me but I still believed he led me on.

My lips had been sealed on the subject of Caleb, but I could tell everyone was dying to know. Even the guys of this clique were gossip whores.

Hannah glanced at me sideways with a smirk on her face. "Your boyfriend is staring at you."

I acted unaffected, even though I was so far from it. My heart was beating like a drum. "He's not my boyfriend anymore."

She raised two perfectly groomed eyebrows. "Well then, your *stepbrother* is staring at you. Scowling, actually."

"He's not my stepbrother anymore, either," I forced myself to say.

She smiled predatorily. "So, it's open season then."

I wanted to claw her eyes out. Rip out what I knew were expensive extensions. I calmed myself down on the inside, trying to match my calm exterior. Giving her a skeptical look, I asked, "Didn't he reject you already?"

Bullseye.

I expected her to strike back at me, instead she grumbled, "He's not that hot anyways."

Seth, who was sitting on my right side and had been listening to the exchange, put his half cent in. "Gianna is my girlfriend now."

Yeah, so I called him early this morning, asked for a ride to school and, *pow,* before we pulled into the parking lot he was my new boyfriend. The kind I'd prefer. The kind that couldn't hurt me.

"Funny," Hannah began and unfortunately continued, "On Monday you were Caleb's girlfriend. You're out of school for three days and now you're Seth's girlfriend."

I flashed her a warning look, the kind that told a bitch she'd better back down. Being the reluctant queen of the school was good for something. *Power*. I could crush her, have her sitting by herself in the library during lunch.

"Nothing funny about it, Hannah. We dated, it's over. Same as it was with me and Josh."

I glanced down the table where Josh was sitting. Him hanging out with this crowd was an unfortunate fact of life. But he could be ignored just as easily as Caleb.

Hannah followed my glance. "Seems like you have two ex-boyfriends pining over you." Josh was staring, too, scowling like Hannah claimed Caleb had been.

Fuck 'em both.

Josh was a sadistic sociopath and Caleb was a narcissistic sociopath. One thought he loved me, the other knew he didn't love me. Caleb only loved himself. There was no room in his heart for anyone else. I didn't need or want either of them.

Josh had never gotten my love.

I'd handed it over to Caleb on a silver platter but he tossed it away.

Like I'd said, fuck 'em both.

Hannah suddenly laughed. "Yeah, you're right. You two are definitely broken up."

"What are you talking about?" I asked, not liking her finding humor in the situation.

Her predatory smile was back, this time all for me. "He's going to town with that chick."

I looked over to where Caleb had been sitting by himself, but no longer was. Matter-of-fact, someone was sitting on his lap. That skank, Desiree, who he'd went on the double date with when I went on my date with Seth. As I saw him kissing her, my eyes darted away.

It hurt too much.

I'd promised myself I wouldn't even acknowledge his existence at school. I wouldn't make the mistake of glancing in his direction again.

My eyes met Seth's. He had a questioning look on his face. I made sure to school my own features. The pain beating inside of me was my own and no one else's business.

How could I have been so wrong about Caleb? How could I still love him so much?

I would not cry. I would not cry. I would not cry.

I'd chant this in my head for the rest of lunch if I had to.

CALEB

I was so busy staring at Gianna, willing her to look at me, that I didn't notice Desiree walking up to me until she was in my lap. When she planted her lips on mine I was startled at first, but then roughly pushed her face away from mine. "Get off!"

She gave me a hurt look, but I didn't buy it. Especially when she tried to kiss me again and I jerked my head back. How could she be surprised by my reaction when I turned down her and her pussy the night we went on our date?

Some sluts never learned.

Fortunately, she moved off my lap. Unfortunately, she didn't completely go away. "So, I heard you and Gianna broke up."

I grunted in response.

"I'm single," she said suggestively.

"That's skanktastic," I replied unenthusiastically.

She narrowed her eyes at me. "What did you just say?"

I looked at her like she was an idiot. "I said . . . that's *whoretastic*."

"What?" she shrieked.

"Sluttastic," I enunciated.

Her face turned red and she swung out an arm to slap me. I ducked, easily avoiding her palm. She marched off and I thought about how genuinely fantastic that was.

What could I say? She'd caught me on a bad day.

I went back to staring at Gianna. My amusement at Desiree's skankness diminished. Seth had his arm around Gianna and I was itching to break it.

What was going on with her? What was going through her mind? How could she pretend nothing happened between us? Did she really love me at all?

Danger! Bad Boy

Jesus fucking Christ! I was acting like such a girl. A stalkerish one at that.

I continued staring her way throughout the rest of lunch period, willing her to look at me. Just one glance would've felt like such an accomplishment.

I loved her so damn much. I wanted to snatch her away from the pretenders, take her back to Vegas, take her anywhere I could have her back. That place didn't exist as long as Julie was hounding us. By the time Gianna was eighteen, it might be too late to get her back.

For the rest of lunch period I kept hoping and she kept not looking my way.

When she said she never wanted to see me again, I hadn't thought she meant it so literally.

CHAPTER NINE

"Friendship often ends in love;
but love in friendship - never."
-Charles Caleb Colton

GIANNA

How could it hurt so much to lose a creep? It defied logic. Why was I cursed to love a heartless asshole?

Everything had come full circle for the cast in the story of my life. I was back in the role I was stuck in before. Ms. Popular Cheerleader who dated the football star. However, the role Josh formerly played was now played by his understudy, Seth.

Caleb didn't exist in my world just like before when I didn't know him.

Unfortunately, he still existed in my mind and heart. As much as I'd tried to cut him out of both of those places, the dissection hadn't taken.

Everything seemed back to normal in Caleb's world, too. He was surrounded by loads of skanky chicks and getting into trouble at school all the time.

This time, however, we'd added a new villain. Not Caleb, but Josh. Back to his stalker ways, he was always there, always watching me. Or should I have said glaring? He wanted the blonde cheerleader, well I could've pointed out a few available and actually interested ones. His psychotic tendencies didn't need to zero in on me.

I never looked Caleb's way. For the most part. Not enough for anyone to have noticed.

Anyways, he hung out with what we used to call *the misfits*; those cool, real people who I totally saw first, dammit!

So, maybe I was envious of that, but then I'd remember that things were as they should be. *Pre-Caleb*. My fake life was more to my liking. Safe from heartbreak (well, at least further heartbreak) and safe from the realness that hurt too much when it got too real.

It'd been three weeks and I was still waiting for it to stop hurting.

Saturdays were a little different now.

CALEB

"What do you mean, she quit the crew?" I asked Dante, who was on the other end of the phone.

"Exactly what I just said. *She. Quit.* She's not even returning Cece's phone calls anymore. My woman is upset about it. And worried about what's up with Gianna," Dante said in an annoyed tone. The fact that my best friend was dating Gianna's best friend was a godsend.

The only other way I got any real information about Gianna was through Chance and I figured stalking a little kid to get info on his big sister was getting kind of pathetic.

"Well, Chance says that she's still going down to Denver every Saturday, so what the hell is she doing?"

"Who's Chance?"

"Uh, never mind." I quickly changed the subject, "So, what are you doing this weekend?"

"Hanging out with Cece. Gonna go watch the crew at a competition this weekend in Colorado Springs."

"Oh, well tell Cece and Taye I said hello." I was ready to get off the phone. I was fucking thrilled for Dante, but his relationship bliss reminded me of my own failure with Gianna.

After I got off the phone with Dante, I just sat on my bed thinking. A solution to the Julie problem was still eluding me. Gianna acted as though I didn't exist and I didn't blame her. From her point-of-view, I was the jerk who used her and ditched her once he got what he wanted.

But I still wanted her.

I wanted her so badly I ached with it. The brief glimpses of her I got at school weren't enough. I wanted all of her like I had her before when she'd been mine. She *still* was mine. She just didn't know it. If only her controlling mother would've realized it too.

That creeper, Josh, hovered near her all the time. I hoped my warning glares kept him off her back. No matter how much I glared at Seth, he still kept close to my girl. Granted, the kid had never done anything wrong, but that didn't mean I didn't want to beat him. If he rubbed Gianna's shoulder one more time or if he even thought about having sex with her, he was a dead man.

Damn, that fucker probably fantasized about it on an hourly basis. I knew I did. The shithead got to hold her in his arms and kiss her lips and I wasn't even allowed to talk to her. If I punched him hard enough, his lips would be too swollen for kissing.

I was tempted to just go down on my knees and beg for her forgiveness. I'd tell her it was all a lie and that I did love her. So fucking much it drove me crazy with wanting her. She wasn't speaking with the crew anyways and they were one of the reasons I'd given in to Julie's threats.

Of course, her mom could still follow through with the threat of sending her away to live with her father or someplace crazy like Siberia.

I just needed to be patient and work out a plan.

I lay back on my bed as a plan that would work continued to elude me.

When the clock turned seven, I hopped up and changed out of what I wore to school that day. Tonight was a home football game. I could watch Gianna cheer on the sidelines for hours. My school spirit had never been better.

Keeping my distance from her at the game was hard. I wanted to snatch her up and run away from everyone. When I wasn't staring at Gianna, I was glaring at every male in the stands who I suspected could possibly be leering at her in her cheerleader uniform. Jeez, the cheerleaders should really be required to wear pants. Loose sweats would've been nice. How many of the grown men here tonight had gotten a hard on for the cheerleaders?

I also scowled at the football players. I hated them all for the clean-cut image they gave the parents, like they were good guys just because they played a sport. Why couldn't parents like Julie realize the only difference between them and me was a jockstrap?

My favorite person to glower at was Seth, the current boy-next-door who Julie approved of.

Yeah, Chance told me things. Freaking loved that kid.

Maybe I should join the football team.

When the game was finally over, I watched Seth rush over to Gianna and pick her up in a bear hug. Besides pissing me off, it made me think about when her nude body was pressed up against mine in Las Vegas. Crap, now *I* was hard!

I discreetly followed Gianna out to her Jeep after the game. I didn't want her to see me, but I wanted to make sure she made it there alright and hassle-free. There were too many potential perverts on the school grounds.

As she passed by my car, she kicked the bumper, hopping around on one foot in obvious pain. She'd done more damage to her foot than my car. I bit my lip to keep from laughing.

Maybe she was hurting as much as me, despite the indifferent face she put on for the world.

After driving past her house and seeing her bedroom light on a half hour later, I drove to my dad's condo twenty minutes away.

Our bachelor pad.

Sparsely furnished, the place was depressing. I sat around moping over Gianna while he sat around moping over Julie. He'd said he didn't understand how you could spend three years with a person and not even know her.

My dad received divorce papers from Julie the other day and his expression when he told me was crestfallen. There might have been tears in his eyes before he went up to his room to be alone. Julie was exorcising my dad out of their lives the same way she had with me.

*****

Saturday night, I called Hailey.

She answered with, "So, did the prom queen dump you?"

"It wasn't like that, Hailey, and is that any way to greet an old friend?"

"I'll take that as a yes. Told you she would realize she was too good for you and kick you to the curb."

"If all you're going to do is make me feel worse than I already do, then I'm hanging up. I thought as an old friend you'd want to console me while we get wasted, but I guess maybe I was wrong."

"Hold up!" She hastily replied. I smiled, knowing Hailey could never resist anything involving alcohol. Sometimes I worried about the girl's future.

"I'll pick you up in an hour," I informed her.

"Okay and, um, sorry about the breakup and whatever."

"That's more like it." I hung up and took a quick shower. Thirty minutes later, I was saying goodbye to my dad then pulling my car out of the driveway.

Approximately thirty more minutes later I was parking in front of Hailey's place, texting her to come down. "Where we going?" she asked as she closed the passenger door.

"I don't know. I've been out of it for awhile. Where do you think?"

She got a sly look on her face. "Well, there's this new club I went to last weekend that was pretty cool."

Therefore, fifteen more minutes later found us entering the new club Hailey had recommended. After dancing to one song, we were at the bar working on the getting wasted part of the night.

I'd drunk three beers before Hailey nudged me and shouted over the music, "I have something to show you."

The thought flashed through my head that she was trying to hook up with me again. Instead of grabbing my dick or something like that, she swiveled around on the barstool she was seated on and pointed out to where one of the club's dancers was up on a low platform.

It was my Gianna.

She was about to be spanked, not in a sexual way but in a way that really fucking hurt. I'd barely noticed the clubs three dancers when we'd entered. Had she been there before?

I looked over at Hailey in time to catch her victorious smile. *She'd known*. She already knew Gianna worked here, that I'd be shocked to see her tonight. What a great friend. Guess Hailey was still a little peeved about my rejection and wanted to hurt me back. This was why I mostly had guy friends. They rarely acted like bitches.

So, what did I do now? This reminded me of the first time I found Gianna at a club. That time had been innocent enough, just dancing with her crew. I'd had no claim on her back then, and blackmail was the only way to get her into my life as more than just a stepsister. I hadn't even known what I was subconsciously doing at the time. The whole list had been an excuse to spend more time with her, get to know her better.

Did I have a claim now? Did I have the right to be pissed off at my ex-girlfriend for dancing at a club?

It wasn't like she was stripping, but she wasn't fully clothed in my opinion, wearing skin-tight black shorts, black furry boots up to her knees and a tight tank top with the club's name printed on it. She was like a dancing promotion and wet dream wrapped into one. The style of dancing wasn't exactly slutty, but then it didn't take much for Gianna to look sexy.

I ordered another beer from the bartender.

I tried ignoring Hailey's taunts. She was really enjoying this.

Although it was another night I could sit and watch Gianna, I didn't appreciate the opportunity. Once again, a bunch of random males got to watch her too. Just great.

Hailey nudged me again. "Just wait. If what happened at the end of the night last Saturday happens again, you won't want to miss it!"

I glared at her, making her laugh. Why did I ever hang out with this bitch?

So this was why Gianna quit the crew, for a job like this that she didn't even need? Didn't she know I'd eventually go to this club and see her here? Had she noticed me here tonight yet? Crap! What if she saw me with Hailey? I planned on getting her back someday and didn't want her thinking I'd hooked up with Hailey while we were apart.

Not that she ever looked my way at school anyways, but she sure wasn't now. She probably hadn't spotted me. The bar area was dark compared to where she was under the lights. Plus, she didn't seem to really pay attention to any of the guys who were loitering around her. She was simply intent on her dancing and the beat of the music.

What did Hailey mean by that end of the night remark? Was that when they poured water on the dancers or something? If so, I was hauling Gianna down from there. I leaned in and shouted in Hailey's ear for her to elaborate but she shook her head, grinning like a maniac. Bitch.

I was drunk but not wasted as planned. Since there was the promise of more in store that night, I figured I shouldn't get too sloshed.

So, at one in the morning I was still sitting at the bar, waiting for the night to end. The club was hopping and people were reluctant to go home. Gianna was still dancing. I was still slowly drinking. Hailey was still being an uninformative bitch, taking off now and then to dance with various guys, mostly just getting free drinks out of them.

The club closed soon, and I hoped my misery would end with the festivities. My hopes weren't very high, though. Life had sucked lately. I'd spilled some beer and was placing napkins on it when Ian walked up.

My archenemy entering the scene made my night complete.

Ian leaned back against the bar, near Hailey and me. She gave him a dirty look he didn't acknowledge. A year or so back he'd fucked her and never returned her calls afterwards.

"Hey, Caleb, isn't that your girlfriend dancing up there?" Ian asked nonchalantly.

I greeted him with, "Fuck off, dickhead!"

"Oh wait, I forgot! That's *my* girlfriend!" He smiled maliciously and moved away towards Gianna.

My Gianna.

I glanced over at Hailey and her matching malicious smile.

Oh, hell no.

I followed Ian, catching up with him just as he grabbed Gianna by the waist and she gripped his shoulders. He helped her down off the platform and onto the floor below. As they were facing each other, smiling, I stood to the side of them, not smiling.

That was when Gianna finally noticed me. She looked startled, so I guess she hadn't known I was here at the club.

CHAPTER TEN

"I got my eyes on you. You're everything that I see.
I want your hot love and emotion endlessly."
-Hold on, We're Going Home by Drake

CALEB

I stared at where Ian's hands were still gripping Gianna's waist. "Getting your fucking hands off her!"

Ian, never one to back down, especially from me, turned to face me, arm now around her waist. "Quit cussing in front of my girlfriend."

Gianna shifted uncomfortably. As she should. She placed a palm on Ian's chest. "Let's just go."

Ian tilted his head down to look at her. "Okay, babe." As if the confrontation was over, Ian, hand at the small of her back, began leading her away.

Instead of heading for the exit, they stopped in front of a set of black double doors with the words *Staff Only* painted in white on them. Naturally, I followed them there. Gianna slipped inside while Ian leaned against the wall to the right of the doors, obviously intent on waiting for her.

As I stopped five feet from the doors Gianna had disappeared through, someone bumped into me from behind. Whipping around, I faced a Hailey with a shit-eating grin on her face.

So smug in her cruelness.

Before dealing with Ian, I had to know something for sure. "Hailey, did you know this would happen tonight?"

Nodding her head, the smile never left her face. I was done with Hailey. Years of friendship had come to an end. I hoped it was worth it for her.

"Where did she go?" I asked Ian.

"To grab her bag and change her clothes," he answered coolly.

"And then what?"

He shrugged the shoulder not leaning against the wall. "Then my princess will probably be hungry. I'll take her out to eat at a diner she likes to go to."

Ian calling her princess, my nickname for her, made me see red, his blood spilling on the floor. She must have told him and he was using the information to taunt me now.

"If she's hungry, I'll be the one to feed her." It was stupid, but the thought of Ian or any other guy doing anything for her, pissed me off.

Ian just rolled his eyes, shaking his head in laughter. "You're a dumbass, Caleb."

"She can't be your girlfriend, Ian. She already has a boyfriend."

Ian lifted one eyebrow arrogantly. "You mean that douche Seth? Well, let's just say I'm in the process of convincing her I'd be a much better boyfriend than either of you."

In my relief, my body relaxed somewhat and I almost smiled. "So, she's not your girlfriend?"

"Yet," he enunciated slowly, grinning confidently. And just like that, I was royally pissed off again. The thought of Ian of all people touching her made me sick.

I despised the bastard, had ever since middle school. I didn't remember exactly what started it, but from the beginning, we'd hated each other. We'd crossed paths at one school or another over the years. We were never at the same one for long, since Ian and I both get expelled often. We'd even messed around with some of the same girls. Hailey, for example. If we ran into each other at a party, it was a coin toss whether or not we'd end up punching it out.

I'd never cared about the other girls. I did care very much about having Gianna in common. It wasn't gonna happen. I stood there with arms crossed, legs apart, bracing myself for the battle to come.

A few minutes later, it arrived. Gianna walked out of the double doors wearing low rise dark blue jeans, a light blue tank top cut just high enough to show the cute belly button piercing that I lusted after and her white Sketchers.

She halted when she spotted me, as if surprised to see me still there.

Catching Ian glance down at her stomach had me wanting to rips his eyes out of his head.

After that first instance of surprise, Gianna totally ignored my presence, not looking my way. She offered Ian a bright smile. "Ready?"

"Sure, *princess.*" Ian emphasized the last word, staring straight at me.

Danger! Bad Boy

"Gianna!" I called out after her as they made their way through the crowd of people. She either pretended not to hear me or she really couldn't over the pounding music. The club was about to close, but spirits were still high as the DJ played one of the last songs of the night.

I trailed them out the exit and could sense Hailey still on my heels, breathing down my neck. I guess she planned to enjoy the show.

As soon as we were out on the street, I yelled, "Gianna!"

She finally acknowledged me, spinning around impatiently. "What the hell do you want, Caleb?"

I stalked over to where she stood next to an annoyed Ian. "What the hell are you doing with your life?"

The bitter look on her pretty face was all wrong. "Why, don't you approve? Do you want to help me become happy again? Should I start writing the list now?"

"Gianna-" I began.

Cutting off what I was about to say, she continued her tirade, now using her fingers to accentuate. "One! Don't ever trust Caleb again. Two! Never have anything to do with Caleb again. Three! Don't ever let Caleb hurt me again. Four! Find some way to forget about what Caleb did and said. Five! Ignore that Caleb is once again screwing anything with a hole."

Ian wiped a hand over his mouth, trying to hide his laughter. Hailey wasn't bothering to muffle her own laughter.

I didn't want Gianna thinking I'd touch another girl. *She* was my only girl. Holding up my right hand, forming a hole with my fingers, I asked, "See this?"

Confused, she nodded.

I spoke slowly, so there was no misunderstanding me. "This is the only thing I've been screwing."

Her mouth dropped open in a combination of shock and embarrassment. She practically spit out the word, "Liar."

Ian had joined Hailey in laughing obnoxiously. "Lame, dumbass."

"Why, Caleb?" Gianna asked suspiciously. "You said yourself you don't love me, so why the celibacy?"

I wasn't about to get into this with an audience, especially not an audience which consisted of my worst enemy before Julie came along and my former friend.

"Can we go somewhere alone to talk?" I pleaded softly.

Gianna seemed unsure, but said, "I don't think that's a good idea, Caleb."

"Neither do I," Ian added.

"No one gives a fuck what you think, asshole!" He had to know how close I was to losing it. We'd rarely been around each other this long without one of us taking a swing.

He pointed an index finger towards Gianna. "She does."

My eyes went back Gianna as she said, "Ian has been a good friend, Caleb."

"A good friend?" I asked incredulously. "Ian is nothing but a conniving bastard!"

Hailey scoffed. "You and Ian only hate each other so much because you're exactly alike. Bad boys with big dicks."

Gianna shot Hailey a black look. "You're such a whore, Hailey."

Hailey moved forward as if about to attack Gianna. I thought about grabbing her by the hair, but restrained myself and grabbed onto her arm instead.

"Don't even think about it," I told Hailey. "Just leave. You got what you came for."

She ignored me, trying to pull out of my grip as she shouted at Gianna, "You think you're so fucking perfect, don't you cheerleader? You think you're better than me, but now you're just another one of Caleb's sluts!"

Not helping my case. I needed to get rid of Hailey before she dug my hole deeper.

Gianna's expression remained calm. "Better than being everyone's slut like you."

I yanked Hailey by the arm to turn her away from Gianna. "Go," I ordered menacingly.

Hailey knew me and my temper. The fear on her face showed me she finally understood she'd pushed me to my limit. Backing up, she was still itching for a fight, but was smart enough to get the hell out a situation where no one was on her side.

With one last look back at us, she screamed, "Fuck all of you!"

Classy parting line executed, Hailey disappeared around the corner of the building and became one less headache for me to deal with.

Taking a deep breath, I held out my hand. "Come with me, Gianna."

Before Gianna could respond, Ian took it upon himself to do it for her. "She's not going anywhere with you, Caleb. She learned that lesson after Vegas."

Just how much had she told the bastard?

It was at that moment I saw it in his face, something he'd been hiding with smugness and arrogance before. Ian really cared about Gianna. He wasn't just trying to get into her pants like with other girls. He wasn't just trying to piss me off. He wanted her for himself.

I should've known. One thing Hailey was right about was the fact that Ian and I were so similar in personalities. I sincerely doubted he had a big dick, though. It couldn't be any more than two inches.

Now, I was worried on a level I hadn't been before. If Ian was serious about her, then he could be trouble. Ian wasn't her stepbrother. Julie didn't know about Ian's disgraceful past. He could hide from Julie that he was just like me. Besides the fact that Ian was from a wealthy family and could give Gianna things I couldn't.

I shook my head to clear it, determination setting in. No, I wouldn't let it happen. Gianna was mine first. She loved me first. She still loved me. Somehow, I'd work it all out. Manipulate the situation any way I had to.

"Gianna," I ground out through clenched teeth, "if you don't want me to kick Ian's ass for the hundredth time, then you need to come with me."

Ian laughed. "As I recall, I've kicked your ass just as many times."

Gianna glanced worriedly back and forth between us. "I don't want you two fighting over me."

"Then you better come with me." I dropped the hand I'd been holding out that she hadn't taken and took a couple steps towards her.

Ian moved to come between us. "Back up, Caleb."

Gianna backed away from both of us. "I see only one solution."

She headed straight for one of the cabs parked along the front of the club, waiting for the club-goers to disperse. Ian went after her, trying to stop her, as I stood there watching, happy enough in the knowledge that she wasn't leaving with him.

I remained standing on the sidewalk, watching her taxi turn the corner, while Ian stalked up to me, getting up in my face. "Leave her alone, Caleb. You had your chance. Now it's mine."

"She's still mine," I informed him, not backing down.

He laughed like it was all a joke. "She told me everything that happened. You couldn't even say *I love you* back to her. Believe me, if Gianna ever says those words to me, I'll be saying them back."

"There was more to it than that, Ian, and once I get it all worked out, she'll know I love her."

Not wanting to waste any more time on him, I walked away, more sober than I'd been thirty minutes ago. As I climbed into my Camaro, I wished I knew where she was headed. If I did, I'd pursue her to have the conversation she'd avoided by running away.

I was in no mood to drive all the way out to my dad's condo and I probably wouldn't pass a breathalyzer, so I drove to the parking garage near my mom's apartment, hoping she wasn't home. I really didn't want to be forced to answer any of her questions.

When I got to the glass doors of the building, I noticed the light above the doors was out. I'd have to tell my mom so she could let the building manager know, if someone hadn't already. I punched in the code, using the screen light from my cell phone to illuminate the keypad and see what the heck I was doing.

I heard a scuffle in the darkness, along the side of the building a few feet away. Thinking I was about to be jumped or mugged, I braced myself.

Until I heard, "What do you want to talk about, Caleb?"

My relief was short-lived as I realize how unsafe she'd been. "What are you doing out here by yourself, Gianna? Someone could've attacked you."

I heard her step closer, enough to make out her form. "I have mace."

"And if there were two of them?"

"I also have a knee that shoots up quickly."

At my exasperated sound, she was silent.

Reaching out to grab her waist, I touched her for the first time in what seemed like an eternity. "Come inside with me."

I sensed her hesitation for a moment, but she went in when I held the door open for her. Once we were in the apartment, I left her in the living room to check my mom's room. The door was open and her bed was empty. She must've been out of town or at a friend's house. Thank god, now we'd have privacy.

Danger! Bad Boy

When I returned to the living room, Gianna was sitting on the couch, gazing across the room at my mom's newest painting. As I neared, she glanced up warily. Feeling elated to be close to her again, I sat down on the middle cushion, right next to her. She popped up immediately to move to the armchair across from me.

"What did you want to talk about, Caleb?" she repeated.

"Us."

She shot me a patronizing look. "There is no *us* anymore, Caleb. You made sure of that."

I was dying to inform her that Julie, her mother, was the one to make sure of it. But, it was too soon. I still had no plan to fight her mom. Instead, I said, "You look beautiful, Gianna."

She rolled her beautiful blue eyes. Her sarcasm didn't bother me. I was just so freaking happy to be in her presence. "So I've been told. Still not so sure it's a blessing."

"You're not just beautiful on the outside, Gianna."

I'd startled her. She looked like she was fighting tears. "Stop it, Caleb. I don't want to hear those kinds of things from you."

"I'm sorry," I apologized, really not wanting her to cry. "Let's talk about you then."

She swallowed, regaining her composure. "What about me?" Her hands were clasped in her lap and I wanted so badly to take them in mine.

"First off, why did you get together with Seth less than a day after we broke up?"

"It's none of your business, Caleb. It has nothing to do with you anymore."

If I wanted to get anything out of her, I was going to have to be honest. "It hurt me, Gianna."

She glanced away, now looking at the painting over my head. "He's . . . safe."

Okay, I could understand that, but it didn't mean it wasn't eating at me. "I see." I knew I shouldn't ask my next question. If she answered a certain way, I'd lose my shit. But I had to ask, "Are you fucking him?"

"God, Caleb," she breathed out in shock. "You shouldn't blurt out stuff like that."

"Are you?" I insisted.

Her eyes held mine. "No."

"And Ian?"

I was beginning to piss her off, by the hard look in her eyes. "Right now, the answer is no."

"Right now?" I asked in disbelief, picturing a bloody Ian again.

"What the hell do you care, Caleb?" Her voice was raised and I was doubly glad my mom wasn't home. "Did you mark your territory and now you don't want anyone else trespassing?"

"You belong to me, Gianna."

Sitting back, she laughed. "I notice you didn't say that I belong *with* you."

"That too," I replied hastily, wishing I could say so much more.

"You didn't feel that way a few weeks ago when you practically ran out of my house."

"I've felt that way since we first met, Gianna."

"Felt what, Caleb? Ownership? Possessiveness? No thanks." She stood up to leave. "I think we've chatted enough for a lifetime. It's time for me to go home."

As she passed me to get to the door, I dragged her down onto my lap.

"What are you doing, Caleb? Despite what you think, you don't own me. You don't have the right to manhandle me!" She fought the hold of my arms.

"No, I don't think I own you, but I know I own your heart."

She stopped struggling, frozen in my lap. Slapping a palm against my shoulder, she burst into tears. "Bastard."

Waiting for the tears to stop, I held her, wishing I could say the words to stop them.

When she quieted down, I forged ahead. "Why did you quit the crew, princess?"

She sniffled. "Because I couldn't stand to face them. They were all right about you."

It hurt she thought that about me. "I'm not that person anymore, Gianna."

"I don't know who you are, Caleb."

I almost said I was the one who loved her. Julie was still in control. With her in control of Gianna, she was therefore in control of me.

Bringing my face down to hers, I whispered, "I don't want you to be unhappy. I don't want you to hurt."

She pushed herself off my lap and onto the cushion next to me. "Too late, Caleb."

Getting up, she was headed for the apartment door. As she reached down to grab her bag, I shot up off of the couch, knowing what I was about to do was stupid, but unable to help myself.

Enclosing my arms around her waist from behind, I buried my face in her neck. "Please stay the night with me, Gianna."

She stiffened and I could've sworn she stopped breathing. "I don't think that's a good idea, Caleb."

"I need you, Gianna." I had no idea how long it would be before I could be near her again. "No sex, I promise. Just let me hold you."

An eternity passed before she relaxed against me. "Okay."

Her tone was heavy with reluctance. Very carefully, I guided her towards my bedroom, coaxing her to where I wanted her. I knew she was frightened I'd hurt her again.

And I was going to try my hardest not to.

CHAPTER ELEVEN

"You know you're in love when you don't want to fall asleep
because reality is finally better than your dreams."
                                                    -Dr. Seuss

GIANNA

I allowed Caleb to steer me down the hall to his bedroom. I guess he could sense my reluctance because he threw me a reassuring smile.

What the hell was I doing? Why did I come here tonight? I felt like one of those pathetic girls who put up with whatever crap the man she loved dished out.

So pathetic, Gianna. He doesn't even love you back!

That was why I came here tonight, because of a misguided hope. I had to admit to myself I'd been hoping if I came to see him, he'd sweep me into his arms and tell me that he didn't mean it, he loved me and couldn't live without me. That he'd been dying without me as much as I'd been dying without him.

So freaking pathetic!

But dammit, I couldn't help it. I was still crazy about him, even if he was only going to hurt me again, I couldn't stay away from him. Just for tonight, I told myself. One more night.

I wanted answers, though. I needed to know why everything went down the way it did.

Caleb pulled me down to sit on the edge of his bed next to him. As he wrapped an arm around my back and brought me close, I asked, "Caleb, were you just using me?"

"Never," he said, kissing my forehead.

God, he smelled good. Sitting this close to him reminded me of the time we were always like this. Always touching, kissing, not getting enough of each other.

I wanted to ask him why he couldn't love me back. I wanted to scream it at him. So, maybe he cared about me, but that wasn't enough.

Wouldn't ever be enough.

A one-sided relationship would have been hell. I closed my eyes and relaxed my head against him, savoring being with him like this again after weeks of deprivation. Just a little bit of heaven.

His thumb was rubbing circles in my back. I soaked up the feeling of his touch. "Gianna, how the hell did you start hanging out with Ian?"

I lifted my face to look up at him. He was clearly mad. Why? If he didn't love me, had thought our relationship had run its course, what did he care who I hung out with?

I answered his question with one of my own. "Is that why I'm here tonight, Caleb? Because you found me with Ian and it's sparked the perpetual competition between you two?"

His laughter was rough and bitter. "Ian is no competition. You're with me because I can't stay away from you any longer."

"Can't stay away from me?" I challenged skeptically. "Caleb, everything that's happened between us is because of you. No one is making you stay away from me but yourself."

His expression was weird. His mouth was opened as if he hesitated to say something. I felt like we were on the verge of something important when he closed his mouth and a guarded look came over him. Deflated, I rested my head back on his chest.

After a minute or two of silence, he finally said, "You didn't answer my question about Ian."

Not looking up at him, I explained, "Ian and I are just friends. The first night I went to the club three weeks ago to apply for the dancing position, he was there. He was very polite and asked if he could have my number. I figured, why not, and we've been hanging out since."

"You used your fake id to get the job?"

"Duh," I teased him, wondering how being with him could still feel so right after everything that had gone wrong between us.

"Are you going to break up with Seth?"

I had to think for a moment. I figured I'd eventually break up with Seth. He was falling too hard for me and I didn't want to hurt him. The reason I'd gotten with him in the first place was no longer valid.

"I probably will soon."

Caleb tensed, holding me tighter. "And then you'll be with Ian?"

I pulled back from him, aggravated that he'd brought up Ian again. "Why do you even care who I'm with, Caleb? You didn't want me."

CALEB

Not want her?

I wanted her in so many different ways it scared me.

I wanted all of her, mind, body and soul. It was making me insane that I couldn't have her. I was daydreaming constantly about murdering Julie. It was getting ridiculous how much I obsessed about finding a way for us to be together. I wasn't able to concentrate in class, especially the two I had with Gianna. My teachers thought I was slacking off and I'd been reprimanded once or twice.

I wondered if I could convince Gianna to meet me here every weekend. Julie wouldn't have to know. Maybe I should have told her about Julie's threats. And maybe Gianna would become so mad with her mom she'd confront her and get shipped off to her dad.

"Gianna, I want to ask you something."

Her facial expression was cautious. "Yeah, Caleb?"

Grabbing her hand, I held it in one of mine. "Can I see you sometimes?"

She looked mistrustful now. "What do you mean?"

I was nervous, needing to state my next words carefully. "Like on Saturdays. Can we spend Saturdays together? Before you got to work and after?"

"Why?" her voice cracked with emotion on the word. "Why are you doing this to me, Caleb?"

I quickly gathered her in my arms, offering her what comfort I could. "I'm not trying to hurt you, princess. I just need to spend time with you."

She jumped up, standing a yard away with her arms crossed. "I don't understand you. You don't love me, you've been okay with our breakup for weeks, but now you need to see me each weekend?"

I ran a hand through my hair, wanting to tear it out in helplessness. "That isn't entirely true. This is so complicated."

She laughed humorlessly. "Tell me about it." She was looking over my shoulder through the open blinds. Through my bedroom window, you could barely make out the top of the Denver skyline. "I should go, Caleb. This is a really bad idea."

Gripping her arm, I brought her back to me. "Please don't go."

"Tell me why I shouldn't," she mumbled against my neck. Her soft lips on my skin made me want more of her.

Everything. Her laughter, her passion, her beauty.

I realized what she was asking, the words she longed to hear. I couldn't let them pass my lips. If I did, how would I explain why it was impossible for us officially get back together?

Fuck, I loved her so much. I skimmed fingers over her face, her lips, down her neck. Someday, I told myself. Someday I'd be able to speak freely of my love for her.

Instead, for now I told her, "Because this is where we both want to be, together."

She slapped her hand against my chest. "You're confusing me, Caleb. The way you look at me sometimes makes me think one thing, then the words you say have me thinking something else. You're hurting me!"

I rubbed her back. "That's the last thing I want to do, baby. Just know this, Gianna, I haven't been with any other girls and I'm not going to be, as long as I can still have you sometimes."

Not entirely true. Even if I couldn't be with her, I had no plans to be with anyone else. I was desperate at this point. I'd tell her just about any lie to get her to agree.

Gianna scoffed, her pretty features looked disgusted. "You mean, if I let you have sex with me, you won't fuck anyone else?"

"That isn't what I meant at all," I backtracked, grinding my teeth in frustration.

Dammit! I couldn't tell her I wouldn't screw any other girls no matter what. For the moment, I needed to use that fear against her to get us back into some sort of relationship.

At the same time, I'd be getting Gianna back one day for real, hopefully soon, and I didn't want any other girls on my conscience. It would hurt my cause if Gianna had any reason to believe I'd messed around with anyone else. Besides the fact I couldn't see myself fucking another girl, period.

I was counting on her territorial feelings to get her agreement.

My dick was practically rubbed raw from thinking about her the past few weeks. Not to mention that being apart from her was fucking with my head.

"What I meant," I explained slowly, "is that I want to spend time with you on the weekends. Whether or not we have sex is up to you. Just being with you is enough for me."

I was given hope by the thoughtful look on her face. I'd said the right thing, thankfully without giving up too much information.

"Caleb, you do realize how pathetic it'd be of me to accept a half-ass relationship from you?"

Kissing her cheek, I forced a lighthearted smile. "It won't be half-ass. You'll have all of me. It'll just be stored up all week for you. You just can't tell *anyone* about it."

An unexpected elbow hit my stomach right before she pushed me down onto the bed, climbing on top of me. All hopes of being ravished were dashed when her angry face hovered over mine.

"Are you freaking serious, Caleb? How stupid do you think I am?" She sat up straight. "Let me get this straight. You want to ignore me all week, see me on Saturdays only and you want me to keep it a secret?" She held both hands over her heart and asked sarcastically, "Oh really, Caleb, can I be your *secret girlfriend*?"

When she laid it all out like that it sounded bad. And strangely funny.

"I just think we should keep it to ourselves."

Both her hands landed on my chest. "What the hell for? So your other hoes won't find out?"

Before she could react, I flipped her over onto her back and pressed my lower body against hers. "I told you already, no other girls. Of course, I'll expect you to cut off all other guys."

She grunted, trying to buck me off her. Being a cheerleader, she was strong, but not strong enough. "Get the fuck off me! I'm not going to be your secret booty call, Caleb! You can go and fuck any girl you want for all I care and I'll be doing the same thing!"

I ground my hips into hers and kissed her forcefully, holding her chin when she tried to turn away. "No one else touches you, Gianna, and you'll meet me here next Saturday or I'll come find you to drag you here."

She screamed in frustration. "I'll be with Ian next Saturday and I'll be fucking him!"

That did it. All rationality flew out of my head because there was only enough room for the extreme jealousy lashing through me. If she fucked Ian, I'd kill him and lock her away somewhere only I could get to her.

I'd fucking kill him and anyone else who touched her.

I started tugging away at her clothes, imagining Ian putting his hands where only I'd touched. I needed to show her I should be the only one touching her. Not until I had her practically naked, only in her panties, did I come back to myself and realize she was crying.

Shaking my head, I got a grip on myself, finally coming to my senses. What the hell was wrong with me?

I cupped her face in my hands, leaning down to press my lips against hers. "Shh, baby, don't cry. I'm so sorry, I would never hurt you. Just, *please*, don't say anything like that again."

Taking a deep breath, she finally stopped crying as I wiped away her tears. The wide-eyed look on her face let me know how much I'd freaked her out.

I used to be normal before I met her. Life was simple. I knew nothing would ever be the same and somehow I didn't care. I couldn't even relate to the guy I was before.

Lifting her slightly, I pulled the comforter back and threw it over her. I stood up to strip off my jeans and shirt, letting them fall to the floor. Joining her under the covers, I took her into my arms.

"Let's just go to sleep, we'll talk about it in the morning."

She didn't answer.

*****

I'd said we'd talk in the morning, but I woke up with a raging hard on and a sexy Gianna curled up against me wearing almost nothing. She was still sleeping sweetly, her beautiful features soft in slumber.

Unable to resist, I lifted up the covers to peek at her body. I needed to be inside her. Hopefully, she'd agree.

I started stroking her body while she slept, rubbing gently, hoping to get her aroused enough in sleep she wouldn't be able to resist me once awake. She groaned sexily, making my hard on twitch in response. It recognized the sound.

Pinching her nipple gently had her coming awake. As her eyelids fluttered, I whispered in her ear, "Morning, pretty girl."

She ran a hand over her eyes. "What are you doing, Caleb?"

"I planned on making love to you."

"You have to actually love me to-"

My mouth on hers cut off what she'd been about to say. I slipped my hand into her panties, stroking her. She forgot her protests and fell into enjoying what I was doing to her. I was enjoying it myself. Watching her pant softly, her pink lips parted, was hot.

I sat up to pull her panties down her legs, my boxer briefs following suit. Stroking myself a couple times, I kissed her breasts, nipping them with my teeth. Gianna's fingers weaved through my hair, gently tugging at it.

Between her legs, I rubbed myself against her then slowly started to enter. She felt as tight as the first time. Fully inside her, I thrusted slowly, savoring the return to paradise. Trying to tell her with my body what I couldn't allow myself to put into words.

Her nails dug into my back as she grazed my neck with her lips. Her head dropped back down onto the pillow, half-closed eyes holding mine as I made love to her. She climaxed, moaning her pleasure, heightening my own.

I could sense her remorse as she settled in my arms afterwards. I had no regrets. We'd come together as we were meant to be. She should feel the same way. "I missed you, Gianna."

She sighed. "Me, too."

I didn't want to have to bring it up, but my need to chain her to me didn't involve propelling her into early motherhood. "I'm sorry I didn't use a condom. I promise I will next time."

"I got on the pill a couple weeks ago, so don't worry."

In my desperation over the past three weeks, one of the plans I'd contemplated was to purposely knock her up. What could Julie do, then? As the father I'd have rights to see my kid, therefore have access to Gianna. Julie would have to admit defeat.

Or at least any sane person would.

Unfortunately, neither of us was ready for a kid and a baby deserved better than that. Tempting, but it was the wrong way to secure a future together.

"Let's take a shower," I suggested, praying my mom didn't come home anytime soon. Getting up, I grabbed some towels, expecting her to follow me. When I glanced back, she was sitting up on the bed, biting her lip. "Come on, princess." I held my hand out for her, mentally willing her to take it.

Danger! Bad Boy

She gave me just enough trust to take my hand. She gave me a little more of her trust when she let me make love to her again in the shower.

Once we were both dressed and Gianna had dried her hair with my mom's blow dryer, we walked to the diner for a late breakfast. I allowed Gianna to order for herself this time.

Grabbing her hand across the table, I asked, "So, when are you going back to the crew?"

Staring down at our hands, she shrugged. "I don't know."

"It makes you happy. You must miss them."

She turned her head to look out the window at the people passing by. "I don't know what I want now."

When this was all over, when I had worked out the Julie problem, hopefully she'd still want *me*.

"Eat up," I told her when our food arrived. She dug into her omelet while I demolished my pancakes. When she didn't finish her hash browns and sausage, I ate those also.

Holding hands as we left, I asked her, "Where's your car?"

She looked unsure and the answer hit me before she said, "At Ian's."

I scowled at her as she held my stare defiantly. "You're not my boyfriend, Caleb. You can't get mad about me having guy friends."

Grabbing her hips, I yanked her against me. "I may not be your boyfriend, but I'm still your man."

She rolled her eyes, smirking. "Hooking up once a week won't make you my man."

I went for an innocent expression. "But, we'll be doing other things, too."

Her look was doubtful. "Like what?"

I pecked her on the lips, wanting to kiss away her doubt. "Whatever you like."

"Shopping?"

I cringed inwardly. "Yes."

"Chick flicks?"

I kept a grimace in check. "Sure, if you want, but you don't like chick flicks."

Her smile was pure feminine glee. "Maybe I've decided they're not so bad. There's this new Emma Stone movie I think you'll love!"

Ugh! I couldn't stand Emma Stone.

She bounced in placed with excitement. I couldn't tell if she was messing with me or not. I wouldn't put it past her to find satisfaction in torturing me. "Oh, and next month there's a new romantic comedy coming out!"

"Yay, romantic comedy," I mumbled weakly. Romantic comedies usually consisted of clumsy chicks falling all over clueless guys. Pure torture.

"It'll be fun," she assured me.

I gave her a naughty grin. "Do I get head from you in the theater?"

She giggled, slapping my arm playfully. "You're such a pervert. Maybe I will if chick flicks turn you on that much."

I planted kisses randomly over her beautiful face. "Being with you in the dark turns me on that much."

"I need to go get my car!" she protested, trying to escape.

Not letting her go, she was forced to give up. "I'll take you to it. How far is it?"

She glanced down the street. "Just a few blocks away."

I grunted unhappily. "That douche lives by my mom?"

"He lives at Riverfront Park," she mentioned nonchalantly.

I whistled. "That high rise is expensive to live in."

"It's pretty nice," she commented vaguely.

Stopping, I turned her to face me. "Is his bedroom nice?"

She let out an exasperated breath. "Quit acting jealous, Caleb. You're not even my boyfriend."

Jerking her hand out of mine, she walked ahead of me. I caught up, falling into step beside her and hooking an over her shoulders.

While we waited at a corner for our turn to cross, she said, "Oh, and his room is like out of a magazine, professionally decorated in different shades of gray."

I noticed she was trying not to smile. "Why the hell would you need to see his room?" I growled irritably.

"I was helping him pick out something to wear to the club."

As if Ian hadn't been dressing himself for years. "He's not the type of person you should hang out with."

Her laugher bubbled out. "He's just like you. Maybe *you're* not the type of person I should be hanging out with."

Too true, not that I gave a damn.

I swooped down to kiss her cheek, not able to get enough of her after so long apart. "You'll come over next Saturday?"

Danger! Bad Boy

Her frown wasn't reassuring. "I don't know yet, we'll see. I'm supposed to hang out with Ian."

I groaned, wishing Ian to hell.

Her face brightened. "Hey, maybe we can all hang out together!"

It was me who was in hell. And Ian was the devil. "Not happening, babe."

We reached the high rise Ian lived in and Gianna insisted on going up to say hello to him. For some reason I didn't understand, she felt bad about running out on him last night. I felt pretty good about it, myself.

She also insisted I go back home instead of waiting on the street for her to come back down. Before we parted ways, I gave her a kiss to remember me by. Watching her get buzzed up by the prick, I managed to stop myself from throwing a tantrum and looking like a dumb fuck.

What a guy put up with in the name of love.

CHAPTER TWELVE

"People are illogical, unreasonable, and self-centered.
Love them anyway."
-Kent M. Keith

GIANNA

The next Saturday night I was back on my designated platform, dancing at the club, attempting to block out the rest of the world. Trying to pretend I was dancing alone, shutting out everyone on the dance floor below.

It was amazing how all of your problems could come crashing down on you at the same time. Or maybe more accurately, they could all show up at your place of work at the same time.

Okay, I was being dramatic. A few *problems* weren't here right now. Thankfully absent, were my controlling mother, my psychotic ex-boyfriend Josh and my newest ex-boyfriend, Seth.

At school on Monday, Seth had taken the break-up harder than I'd thought he would. After spending last Saturday night and Sunday morning with Caleb, I knew it was wrong of me to lead Seth on any longer. Even though my heart had never been in the relationship, technically I'd cheated on Seth.

Not that I ever planned on letting him know. I felt guilty enough as it was. I'd feel worse if he thought I was a slut.

I chose to see the breakup as setting him free to be with someone who deserved him. He was a nice guy and would make a good boyfriend to another girl. Unfortunately, Seth saw the breakup as losing the only girl he wanted. His watery eyes and pleading had made me feel uncomfortable.

When I'd broken up with Josh, it'd been so easy. He'd acted like a creeper, so I didn't have to be considerate at all when I dumped him. With Seth, however, I'd hugged him, asking if we could still be friends.

When his answer was yes, I was surprised by how relieved I'd felt. I genuinely liked Seth as a person. It was too bad I couldn't love the nice guy instead of being cursed to love the baddest of bad boys.

Although, Ian could give Caleb a run for his money in the bad boy department.

Seriously, they should get along better than they did.

Josh was still giving me stalker eyes most days at school. The guy seriously needed a shrink to dispense some meds. My mom could probably make some recommendations.

She had been driving me crazy all week. Mother's intuition had kicked in with a vengeance and she somehow sensed the return of Caleb in my life. She was always asking me if I'd talked to Caleb, demanding I stay away from him.

She knew about my job, but didn't question how I'd gotten it. She'd been so relieved Caleb and I had broken up, she was willing to agree to anything. When I hadn't come home last Saturday night, I'd told her I spent the night at Cece's.

I was tempted to see how my mom would react if I brought home one of the potheads from my school. Maybe find a guy with more piercings and tattoos than Caleb. Or a ten page rap sheet.

As for Caleb, well, he was still his usual bipolar self. Confusing the hell out of me and all the while making me crave more of him. If only he weren't so hot and I wasn't crazy about him.

Last weekend was unexpected, but maybe subconsciously inevitable. He swore there hadn't been any girls since me and there wouldn't be as long as I gave him his one day a week. The feminist buried deep down inside somewhere wanted to smack him for that one.

The DJ changed songs and I changed my mode of dancing. The pop song previously playing was alright, but the R&B song playing now was one of my favorites. Losing myself in the music, I momentarily let go of my problems.

Someone shouting up at me jolted me out of the zone. Trying to be heard over the music was a guy I didn't know. It was so tacky when guys tried to hit on a club's dancers. In response, I did what I'd been instructed by the manager to do. I smiled at him, blowing him off as I continued dancing.

The reason I took a job at this club and not another was because the owners didn't expect us dancers to dress like hookers. Tonight we wore black motorcycle boots, red shorts and black tank tops with the club logo on the front. It could definitely be worse. As long as I was decently covered and could move in the outfit, it didn't matter to me.

The next song was the dance version of a Katy Perry track that reminded me of Caleb. Just what I needed, another reminder of my not-boyfriend, but not-quite-ex-boyfriend.

I would've liked to think I'd been avoiding him all week, but I hadn't. Caleb didn't come near me at school, call me after school or show up at my house. I got no opportunity to avoid him like he deserved.

It sucked and was totally deflating.

What was his deal?

He didn't want to be together, only wanted to see me once a week and didn't want to be with anyone else. It made no sense. Here he had a girl who was crazy about him, admittedly loved him and was simply asking for his love in return.

But, no, all he wanted was some half-ass non-relationship.

I'd been dissecting it all week and I didn't think I had it in me to give him what he'd asked for. It was just plain sad.

So, maybe I'd found a rose under my windshield wiper on Tuesday and a newly released Blu-ray I'd been wanting in my locker on Friday. These little gifts during the week didn't earn him my time on the weekend.

So, maybe I was pathetic enough that they'd brought a smile to my face. It didn't mean I was pathetic enough to let him think he owned me.

Accompanying the rose had been a note that said, "Can't wait till Saturday."

Along with the movie had been a post-it that suggested, "An option for Saturday night."

The fact he'd stood in the stands at the football game last night, watching me cheer, didn't mean anything either. Even if his eyes had been on me instead of the game every time I'd glanced his way.

Lying in bed at night, I obsessed over what his real motives were. I was losing sleep and being tired at school sucked big time. I couldn't figure him out.

He didn't love me, but refused to let me go.

He didn't want me as a full-time girlfriend, but was desperate to see me once a week.

In my most hopeful moments, I let myself believe he did love me but was too afraid to tell me. That the reason he wasn't dating other girls was because he didn't want anyone but me. Maybe a player needed time to adjust to falling in love. Maybe he did love me, but was too stubborn to realize it.

If that were the case, I could wait patiently for him to come to his senses and utter those three little words.

My new confidant, Ian, believed differently. So, yeah, my new best friend was Caleb's worst enemy. Ian provided me with a weird insight into the minds of guys like them. Had I planned to become best buddies with a guy Caleb hated? Nope. Was I enjoying how much it annoyed Caleb? Maybe a little.

Ian was actually a lot of fun to hang out with. Spending time with him reminded me of the early days with Caleb, before we entered into a rollercoaster relationship.

Thinking of Ian and Caleb made me smile. They were so much alike in so many ways. Both of them made me laugh with their irreverent senses of humor. Anytime I went anywhere with Ian, there was a chance we'd run into past conquests. So like Caleb.

Still, in some ways Caleb and Ian were way different. As where Caleb was the free spirit, fun-loving type of guy, Ian was the exact opposite. When Ian cared about someone, he would do anything for them. But, he was often cold toward anyone not on his short list of friends.

It made me glad I didn't fall into the non-friend category. I sensed a cruelness in Ian I hoped was never aimed in my direction.

I'd have to suck it up and go crawling back to Cece and the crew soon.

The first Saturday after Caleb and I had ended things, I didn't go to ballet class that morning, but I did drive down into Denver. I'd skipped practice with the crew and the competition we had that night. After receiving texts and voicemails from them all night and throughout the next day, I'd finally texted Jared and Cece. I'd explained that I needed time alone.

I was beginning to feel like a shitty friend.

That same Saturday night, I'd come to this club, applied for the dancing position, ran into Ian, auditioned the next day and here was I was.

I felt guilty about letting down the crew, but in my misery after the breakup, I hadn't felt like I could be around them. It was in no way their fault, of course. In fact, they'd warned me to be careful about Caleb. Stupidly, I hadn't listened.

I'd planned to go back to them and patch things up when I was ready. When I got my head on straight again and wasn't acting like a coward, if they still wanted me.

So, perhaps not all my problems were here tonight, but half of them were.

Caleb.

Ian.

The crew.

Time had run out and it was time for me to be brave.

Caleb had basically said I'd have no choice, that I'd be hanging out with him every Saturday after work. But I was feeling pretty feisty in my cool boots. If he came any closer to my platform, I'd be tempted to kick him to prove just how much choice I had.

So, maybe every part of my being was missing him like crazy and craving his attention. It didn't mean I had to make it easy for him. I wasn't a dog to come running with a leash in my mouth. The fact I'd brought in my bag tonight the Blu-ray movie he'd given me wasn't a sign of surrender.

Ian came with me here tonight and I saw Caleb walk in about an hour ago. Looking sexy as hell and getting hit on by anything wearing a bra, and sometimes not wearing one, he seemed content to wait out my shift. I'd have liked to punt some of those girls in the face with my kickass boots.

Caleb hadn't ventured near me, but I could see him chatting with some girl at the bar. I was jealous even if she wasn't very cute. When he followed her onto the dance floor, my jealousy skyrocketed. One badass motorcycle boot to the face coming right up. Make that two.

While I glared in the direction of Caleb and the *so*-not-cute girl dancing, I didn't notice Ian was standing directly below me. A light brush against my calf alerted me to his presence. Right before I glanced down at him, I noticed Caleb scowling in our direction. I graced Ian with my warmest smile. Returning it, Ian tapped his watch to let me know my break was coming up.

During my break, one of my other problems would be performing. I knew there was a chance my crew would show up at this particular club eventually. I just hadn't expected it to be so soon.

I wasn't looking forward to facing them. I'd seen them slipping into the club earlier, immediately being ushered by the entertainment coordinator into the back rooms. They were probably busy changing, warming up and doing a last minute pep talk.

The track ended less than a minute later and I gripped Ian's shoulder to jump down onto the floor. Picking up my bottle of water from the platform ledge, I chugged down what was left of it. The other two dancers were also taking their breaks now that the entertainment was about to start.

The lights dimmed and new music began. I allowed Ian to grab my hand and pull me closer to where the crew would perform near the stairs leading up to the DJ booth. Over the first beats of the music, the DJ announced them and multi-colored lights rotated to shine on them.

As I watched their performance, I felt an ache in my chest. They looked great and had come up with a new routine. I got a small sense of satisfaction from the fact I hadn't been replaced, leaving Cece as the only girl in the group.

Seeing them dance, I realized how much I missed them. How wrong I was to unfairly push them out of my life when Caleb had hurt me. I guess I was just taking it out on my friends at a time when the cause of my pain wasn't around to lash out at.

Ian stood on my left as someone shouted in my right ear, "You're going back to them aren't you?"

I turned my head to the side and came face to face with Caleb. Our lips were less than an inch apart. I shouted back at him, "How do you know?"

He leaned into me again. "Cause I know *you*, Gianna. I can see it on your face."

Whatever. I gave him a dirty look. "What do you want, Caleb?"

He shrugged. "Just killing time until our date."

"I'm hanging out with Ian tonight," I told him smugly. Let's see how much he wanted that *date* now.

He glowered past me at Ian. "Do we have to?"

My answer was an evil grin.

Scowling, he stalked off, obviously not happy.

My grin became genuine.

I watched as Caleb disappeared into the crowd then turned my attention back to the performance. When it ended, I snatched Ian's hand to take him to be introduced to my friends. Ian was either oblivious to Caleb's earlier presence or he just chose not to acknowledge him. Tonight should be interesting.

As I walked up to Cece first, she squealed and pulled me into a hug. Her thin arms practically squeezed me to death. "Gianna, where the heck have you been?"

God, I was so ashamed. I was a big fat coward and a terrible friend. "Just going through things, but I'm better now."

My sweet friend looked sympathetic. "Yeah, I know. Dante told me about your and Caleb's breakup. Sorry."

"It's okay," I told her, not wanting to get into it right now.

"Hey, you should come to our house tonight! Jared and I are having everyone over after this." Cece was bouncing up and down at the idea of me returning to the fold. It was like being friends with Tigger. She finally noticed Ian. "Who's he?"

I smiled, eager to introduce them. Cece's bubbly personality would probably grate on Ian's nerves. "This is my friend, Ian. Ian, this is Cece."

Ian gave her a polite nod and she waved at him like a dork, saying, "Yo!"

Cece bounced again. "He can come too."

"I have to go back to work, but I'll definitely be there later tonight," I promised her, feeling much better now that I planned to reconnect with my closest friends.

"Work?" Cece's forehead wrinkled in confusion.

I pointed at the obvious logo on my chest. "I work here. Dancing."

Her eyes shot wide. "Oh!"

Noting the other dancers taking their places, I reached out to squeeze her hand. "See you later?"

She smiled happily. "Yeah."

The DJ already had a new song playing. Returning to my platform, I lost myself in the music once again. This time, much less stressed.

112

CHAPTER THIRTEEN

*"If I could choose between loving you and breathing
I would use my last breath to say I love you."*
-Anonymous

CALEB

I was so going to end up in a fight tonight. I just knew it. The question was, whose ass would I be kicking? I looked at Jared where he was leaning in a doorway across the room, glaring at me. My eyes darted over to Ian, where he was working his meager charm on Cece, trying to get in good with the best friend. As long as they didn't try to jump me together, I'd be fine with taking them on one at a time, and taking my time with each one of them.

Jared must have felt so smug right about now. Since I'd supposedly proved him right and broken Gianna's heart. What about my heart? Pretending I was unaffected by the breakup had been hard on me. But no, I was the player and they didn't have feelings, they didn't love.

And Ian was a whole other mess. He was currently playing the part of the sensitive guy friend. He just wanted what was best for Gianna, wanted to be her friend, blah, blah, blah. Yeah right. Did he pursue her just to irritate me? Okay, so maybe that was a little vain of me, since Gianna was one of the most desirable girls either of us had ever met. Definitely the best girl we'd ever competed over. Plus she was cool as hell, especially when she was happy.

Look at him over there, sucking Cece into his web, like a fucking spider.

I did nothing to hide my smile when Dante came over and put his arm around Cece, practically snarling at Ian. My boy, Dante, knew all about my never-ending rivalry with Ian. Sometimes I'd steal the girl Ian was messing around with and sometimes he'd steal the girl I was messing around with. The girl had never been important before, just a means for us to fuck each other over.

Gianna *was* important.

She wasn't one of those meaningless skanks or bimbos we'd fought over in the past. I intended to make that clear to Ian tonight. He messed around with her and he'd be hurting. I didn't care if I had to fight dirty.

I glanced around the living room. Gianna was still nowhere in sight. After she got off work at the club, I hopped into my car and followed her and Ian to Jared and Cece's house. Yeah, so I was a little more than pissed she'd gone with Ian in his car. If she hadn't been in the car with him, I might have rammed the back of his yuppie black BMW.

My plans for tonight had included myself and Gianna, alone, cuddling on a couch somewhere. Quality time type of stuff. Not me being forced to spend time with her crew, who probably hated me for hurting her and being the catalyst in her dropping them for a few weeks. I was the asshole here.

And on top of it, I had to look at Ian's ugly mug all night.

I was so close to kidnapping Gianna and taking her somewhere where we could be alone and talk. The talking would involve me outing her mom's blackmail scheme and telling her she was my everything. That I loved her as much, if not more than she loved me. The conversation would be followed by her showing me how much she loved me back.

Oh yeah, that'd probably be the best part.

I'd thought it before and I thought it again, I should have never brought her back from Las Vegas. We could've lived off my savings until we found work. I laughed derisively to myself, imagining what kind of work we'd find there, with no real experience. Gianna would've probably ended up as a stripper and me, well . . . nothing legal.

According to haters like Julie, I'd never amount to anything. I was just a juvenile delinquent on his way to being a career criminal. So maybe a place like Vegas was perfect for me, lots of cons and crime going down every day.

Some redheaded slut one of the crew brought back from the club was giving me sex eyes from two sofa cushions over. I'd been doing my best to ignore her, but she was at this time in the process of scooting her unwanted drunkass next to me.

Ian smirked in our direction and exited into the kitchen. I should so sick her on him. The words *hot mess* came to mind as I glanced sideways at her. I imagined her passing out with her head on my lap at the same moment Gianna walked back into the room. With the way my life had been going, that would be just my luck.

I scooted over the one inch I had to spare before my right thigh was flush with the armrest. She turned her head and opened her mouth to speak; the smell of beer on her breath was strong. "What's your name, hottie?" With her hand on my thigh, near my junk, I felt kinda victimized.

Seriously? I mean, *seriously?* Please go away.

I smiled at her blankly. "No hablo inglés." Good thing I paid attention in Spanish class.

Her mouth dropped open. "What?"

"Usted es una puta." I smiled inanely at her again.

She gave me a confused half-smile. "Did you just say that I'm pretty?"

Oh brother, this girl was muy estúpida. I cleared my throat and tried not to laugh in her face. "Actually, I just said that you're a slut."

I should've seen the slap coming, but I was distracted by Ian reentering the room with a beer in his hand. He witnessed the slap, laughing obnoxiously, but I gave him payback. Looking back at the girl, I said in a cajoling tone, "I'm sorry, I'm a jerk." Then I pointed over to Ian, "See that guy over there?" At her unsure nod, I continued, "Well, he's a really nice guy. You should go talk to him."

She licked her lips. "He's a hottie too." Oh yeah, honey, eat him alive.

"Sure, if you say so," I mumbled as she staggered to her feet in her ridiculous platform shoes and wobbled over to bother a person who couldn't be more deserving of her attention.

Less than a minute later, Ian was getting a slap *and* a kick from the hot mess. I was almost jealous. Was I not worthy of a kick to the shin also? I almost felt guilty for siccing her on Ian. I'd break a girl's heart with a smile, but he'd do it with a sneer.

After the girl stomped off in her heavy shoes, Ian sauntered arrogantly over to me, sitting at the other end of the couch. "When have I ever been interested your castoffs, Caleb?"

"Do you consider Gianna one of my castoffs, douche?" I asked him with one eyebrow raised.

Ian's face became less arrogant and more, dare I say it, soft. "Gianna's different. Better than all those other bitches." He met my eyes again. "Much too good for you."

"Even much more too good for you then, jerk." I glared at him, resenting everything about him.

"I want her," Ian informed me as if I gave a crap. As if it settled the matter.

"You want her to piss me off, prick," I said through clenched teeth.

He looked at me in surprise and I was annoyed that I couldn't figure out whether or not it was genuine. "This isn't about you and me, and our childish rivalry, Caleb. I want her for herself, not because it would upset you." He smiled evilly. "Of course, the fact it would piss you off would be a bonus."

"I don't have to listen to your shit. I'm going to go find Gianna, dickhead." Leaving the living room, I went in search for her in the direction I saw her go when we first got here. She'd still been in her work clothes and had gone down the hallway to Cece's room to change.

When I reached Cece's room, the door was slightly ajar and the light was off. Pushing it open, I switched the light on. Gianna's duffel bag was there on the bed, but no sign of her.

I followed the noise to the back of the house and peered through the back screen door. The backyard patio lights were on and I saw Gianna standing amongst members of the crew. Opening up the screen door, I stepped outside and shut both doors behind me. The weather was starting to get cold with fall ending and I was sure the Ramirez family would appreciate their guests not upping their heating bill.

Unfortunately, Jared had made his way back here and he, along some of the other guys, were showing Gianna a few dance moves. Catching her up on what she'd missed out on, I was sure. She had a silly grin on her face, so I didn't have the heart to interrupt yet by demanding her attention. Pulling back a patio chair from the table, I took a seat.

I guess the sound of my chair scraping against the cement alerted everyone to my presence because, when I looked up, most everyone's eyes were on me. I had to say, some of the looks the guys were giving me weren't very nice at all. Shame on them.

Gianna said something to the group and started walking across the grass to me. She looked great, wearing a pair of tight jeans, the same black motorcycle boots from the club and a blue thermal hoodie. Her dark blond hair was in a pony tail and I imagined letting it down later tonight and running my fingers through the soft strands. I imagined touching her all over, actually.

She smiled sweetly when she reached me, but then the acidic words came out of her mouth, "Hey, where's Ian?"

I tried to keep a straight face as I lied, "Last I saw, he was making out with some wasted girl from the club."

"Really? I was beginning to think he was gay." Her face was all scrunched up in confusion.

At her words, it was like I fell in love with her all over again.

I couldn't play it cool any longer, I busted out laughing. "Why did you think that?"

She shrugged. "I dunno. He's been so sweet and sensitive, lately."

So Ian's plan was backfiring. I mentally rubbed my hands together in glee. All the better for me. When I glanced back up at Gianna, she was grinning. Narrowing my eyes at her, I snapped, "What?"

"I can't believe you fell for that. I just wanted to see the look on your face, Caleb. Ian is so *not* gay he could be your long lost manwhore twin." Gianna was giggling in delight at messing with me.

I grabbed her by the waist and pulled her down onto my lap. "Come here, bratty girl."

She was laughing hysterically, trying to catch her breath. "Tell the truth, Caleb. Did the thought of Ian being gay put that happy look on your face 'cause it means you have me all to yourself tonight, or was it something else? Hmm? Were you hoping I'd put in a good word for you?"

"Shut up brat," I murmured before bringing her face up to mine for a kiss. Ah, this was what I'd been dying for. I needed my fix. "I've missed you, princess."

Opening her eyes, she gazed up at me. "Did you miss me so much you called me on Tuesday? Did you talk to me in school on Wednesday? How about Thursday?" She shook her head. "I thought not."

She hopped off my lap and sat in a chair next to me, eyeing me unhappily. I ran a hand through my hair in frustration and helplessness. "I told you I have my reasons."

"Yes," she said slowly, "But you haven't informed me of what those reasons are. Considering the fact I'm the one who's getting hurt, don't you think I'm the one person who you should be explaining them to?"

This wasn't working. This whole situation, plan of action, was only succeeding in placing distance and resentment between Gianna and me. If I continued on this path, Julie would win in the end because Gianna would become so bitter she wouldn't want anything to do with me anymore.

Looking over her shoulder to where I was receiving a few warning looks from her friends, I took a deep breath. The time had come to take the risk. "Gianna, if I promise to tell you everything, will you leave this party with me right now?"

Her mouth parted in shock and her eyes bugged out. "Really? Everything?"

Standing up, I grabbed her hand and brought her to her feet. "Yes, come on."

I pulled her along with me through the back door and into the house, stopping by Cece's room to pick up her bag and going into the kitchen to exit through the garage. Therefore, successfully circumventing Ian in the living room.

"I should really tell Ian I'm leaving," Gianna said as I continued to drag her along.

Opening the passenger door of my car for her, I shook my head. "I can't be positive, but I'm pretty sure Ian can read. Text him."

Shutting the door for her, I rushed around the car, picturing someone coming out the front door to halt us, Ian, Jared, even Cece, and threw her bag into the backseat before starting the car.

And we were off. The house was in my rearview mirror, just like I'd been dreaming of for the past hour. I drove a few minutes away until we were at the park where I first asked her to be my girlfriend. Good memories. Well okay, at the time I'd kind of *told* her she was going to be my girlfriend. The parking lot on this side of the park was empty. I turned off the ignition and turned in my seat to face her.

Even in the dark, I could see how sad she looked. Her eyes were shimmering with tears. She was remembering, too. I was so fucking tired of having to watch her cry while I was helpless to make it better. Her tears were breaking me.

Desperate to erase every bad memory between us, I lifted her up and helped her into the backseat, following right after. Dragging her into my body, I began tugging at her clothes in a frenzy. I had her down to nothing in less than two minutes. At the same time I was pushing her onto her back with one hand, I was unzipping my jeans with the other. I entered her roughly, knowing she was ready for me. Thrusting in and out of her wildly, I kissed any part of her within reach of my mouth.

Like an emotional dam that'd been broken, I was saying against her skin, her lips, her cheek, over and over again, "I love you. I love you. I love you."

She climaxed more intensely than ever before. After watching her, I allowed myself to follow. Collapsing on top of her, I mumbled, "I'm sorry."

My heartbeat was taking its time slowing down. Fucking her was amazing.

Instead of recriminations for my barbaric behavior, she lightly ran her fingers through my hair and whispered hoarsely, "I love you, too."

Despite all the anxiety caused by our uncertain future, a part of me that'd been wound up tight for weeks was finally able to relax.

CHAPTER FOURTEEN

"Passion makes the world go round.
Love just makes it a safer place."
-Ice T

GIANNA

"Oh my god! Stop! Stop it, Caleb, behave!" I shouted, jumping off the bed to race to the living room. I could hear him laughing as he followed me. Grabbing two pillows off the couch, I whirled around to face him. I chucked them at him, one after another. The first totally missed him, but the second hit him smack on the face. His way-too-handsome face that I adored.

The pillows had failed to stop him. He just smiled and grabbed a hold of me, pinning my arms within his so I couldn't get away. I struggled anyways. After all, number one rule for a girl? Never make it too easy for the guy.

"You're mine now."

I ducked my head against his bare chest to hide my smile. "For the moment, Caleb."

"For always, princess."

Damn gotta love a tamed bad boy. Best of both worlds, sweet and wild.

Thinking of last night, how wonderful it was, how wonderful *he* was, I sighed. "Tell me again."

He put his hand under my chin to lift my face up to his. Kissing me softly on the cheek, he whispered, "I love you, Gianna."

And just like that, I was feeling all girly and giddy. Ah hell! The boy owned me, body, heart, soul, every piece of me. Not that I'd ever tell him that.

I smiled coyly at him, eating it up. "Why?"

Looking a little confused at my question, he muttered to himself. "Why do girls always have to ask why?"

Exasperated, I demanded, "Because I want to know!"

He laughed, shaking his head as if I were ridiculous. "I just do."

I struggled again until he let me go. Why did boys always have to be so difficult? "Not good enough, Caleb. I *am* a girl and after you denying loving me for so long, forgive me, but I'm a little insecure about it."

His body fell back onto the couch as he lazily sat down. I glanced at where the top button of his jeans was undone then quickly back up at his face. The grin he sported let me know he'd seen where my eyes had wandered.

"Why?" I demanded again.

"'Cause you look so sexy in your little cheerleader uniform?" His eyes roamed up and down my body, as if picturing it in his head.

I shrugged, nonchalantly saying, "I can accept that, since I love you because of your cool car."

"Brat." He chuckled, reaching out to grab the waistband of my sweats, pulling me onto his lap.

"Okay, okay," I laughed the words. "It's 'cause you have a cute butt."

He palmed my own bottom and squeezed. "You too, baby."

Pushing against his chest, I whined, "Caleb, you're supposed to be offended."

His lips were kissing my neck, making me squirm. "Why should I be offended? I know how fine I am."

"Hmm," I hummed. "You're alright looking."

"You too, Gianna. You'll do," he teased then pulled back to look at me seriously. "Why do *you* love *me*?"

Caleb needing reassurance? Interesting. Until I suddenly felt a little on-the-spot. So, this was what a guy felt like when his girlfriend acted all needy. "Um," I began.

Not cutting me any slack, his expression was skeptical. "Um?"

"Because," I began again, at loss for words and feeling a blush coming on. "Because," I said slowly."

"Because?" he echoed, clearly amused now.

I scowled at him. "Because you care about me." The assertion gave me strength and it became easier to continue. "Because you understand me. Because you're so good to me." I punched him lightly on his chest. "When you aren't lying about loving me and ignoring me at school."

He scoffed in disbelief. "Believe me, I was never ignoring you." Brushing a strand of hair behind my ear, he said sweetly, "I'm always aware of you."

I smiled in satisfaction, adding, "And because you love me." Jumping up and down a little on his lap, I prompted, "Okay, my turn. Why do you love me?" My hands were clasped together in anticipation.

He laughed softly. His hazel eyes had a sexy look in them. "Alright, alright." With a serious face, he said with meaning. "Because you look so hot in your cheerleader uniform."

"Caleb!" I whined in annoyance. "Be serious!"

Placing both of his warm hands on either side of my face, he said with a light smile on his lips. "I love you because you're you. Because underneath all that physical perfection is a vulnerable, beautiful soul who needs me and loves me back. Who sees the good in me."

"You *are* good," I stated sincerely. *And vulnerable too*, I thought to myself.

He visibly shuddered. "Enough of all this mushiness. Let's have sex!"

I laughed loudly as he picked me up off the couch, intent, I suspected, on carrying me back to his bed. My intentions were otherwise, not that my hormones weren't raging as much as his. Okay well, almost as much. Wiggling like crazy, I jumped out of his arms before he made it to the hallway.

"Wait, we need to talk seriously." I held up a hand to ward him off.

His look was impatient. "What's there to talk about? I love you, you love me, now let's have sex."

Hands on my hips, I glided around him and sat down on the couch, by myself this time. "There's plenty to talk about, Caleb Morrison."

"Like?" he pouted, clearly disappointed.

I stared at him thoughtfully. Where to begin? Everything was such a mess and unlike him, I couldn't just live in the moment and jump into bed, forgetting about all of our problems.

Last night was wonderful, a dream come true in so many ways. Caleb had made love to me, well more like ravished me in his car, but it was still romantic because he'd told me he loved me.

Some guys might declare their love in more romantic ways, but I knew who Caleb was and I loved all of him. For Caleb, that *was* romance.

122

But even when something was a dream come true, it didn't mean everything was perfect. I believed Caleb when he told me he loved me. Looking back at the past couple months, I could see it was there all along.

There were still issues that bothered me, though.

Thank god we had the time alone at his mom's apartment to discuss our relationship. My mom wouldn't expect me home until this afternoon and it was barely ten in the morning.

"Sit," I told him, then added, "Please."

Looking disgruntled, he complied and took a seat in a recliner across from me. Crossing his arms over his chest, he asked cautiously, "What do you want to talk about?"

I licked my lips nervously. "You told me last night about how my mom threatened you with sending me to Texas if you didn't break up with me and that's why you had to hurt me, but you didn't explain the most important part."

"I told you everything that happened and why I did what I did." Looking at the floor, his face was a mask of concentration. With his head slightly tilted down, a lock of black hair had fallen over one eye. He glanced up at me. "So, what's the most important part?"

Even knowing now that he loved me, I was still hurt. Trying not to cry *again*, I asked, "Why did you choose to break my heart instead of telling me the truth?"

He shifted uncomfortably in his seat and looked guilty. Sounding reluctant, he admitted, "I guess I just panicked. When your mom threatened to ship you off to your dad or even farther away if she had too, I gave in because she sounded completely serious and I had no doubt she would do something so horrible. I thought I'd figure something out eventually so we could be together. But for the time being, you would at least still be near."

Damn, I was about to cry anyways. Appearing panicked, Caleb rushed over to pull me into his arms. "Shh, don't cry. It'll be okay. We'll just have to be careful for awhile."

Wiping at my tears with impatient fingers, I tilted my head back to look up at him. "Are you sure you didn't give into her so easily because you were afraid of something else?"

He didn't meet my gaze when he asked, "What else could I have been afraid of?"

Breaking away from his embrace, I paced across the room before whipping around. "Me!"

With guarded eyes, he asked, "Why would I be afraid of you?"

I hugged myself in a defensive position, peering down at the floor. "Were you trying to protect me or were you trying to protect yourself, Caleb?"

"I don't know what you mean." His words were tense.

"Don't you, Caleb? Think about it! You could have told me and done exactly what we plan to do now, hidden our relationship. Instead, you lied and said you didn't love me, you hurt me and for weeks ignored me. I know what my mom said was part of your reason, but I think there was another reason, too."

He was getting mad, but I didn't care. I wanted, *needed*, the truth. "I think you latched onto that excuse to distance yourself from me. Our trip to Las Vegas was . . . intense. I told you I loved you and you panicked for that reason, also. The player in you came out, the fear of commitment. I think my mom was an excuse to run away from me and your feelings."

The look of shock, followed by a look of comprehension made me want to cry more.

And I did.

Maybe he hadn't realized it himself, but subconsciously, he had still been afraid of everything falling in love meant.

Rushing out of the room, I could hear his steps on the hardwood floor behind me. I tried to shut his bedroom door, but he was already there stopping me. Instead, I went over to the window and stood there with my back to him, looking down at the street below. Silent tears streamed down my face.

I was so fucking sick of crying.

I could feel him behind me, just standing there. "Gianna, I love you."

My shoulders were hunched, my arms crossed, hands gripping my elbows. "How do I know you won't get scared and run away again?"

His voice was husky. "You can count on me, Gianna. I'm completely and fully committed to you. I'm promising forever, if that's okay with you. You'll be eighteen in about a year and a half and we'll tell your mom to go to hell."

So, it'd taken a few weeks apart, but love had won out. He wasn't afraid anymore and I didn't have to be either.

Turning around, I launched myself into my arms. His arms automatically enclosed me, offering a safe place. I gave in to what we both wanted, letting him guide me over to his bed.

CALEB

Driving back to the suburbs and having to drop Gianna off down the block from her house really pissed me off. We shouldn't have to hide our love like it was a crime. We weren't doing anything wrong. Aside from a little premarital sex, of course.

Halfway to my dad's condo, my cell rang. Hoping it was Gianna, I checked the caller id. It was my mom. I hit the button to answer, "Hello?"

"Caleb," she said in a stern voice.

"Yes, mother?" We both knew my polite act was bullshit.

"I just got home and found a pair of panties on your bedroom floor."

I choked on a laugh. "It's not what you think."

"Are you going back to your old ways?"

"Definitely not," I assured her, not wanting to have this conversation with my mom. "They're Gianna's."

She let out a big breath over the line. "I know I shouldn't be relieved, but somehow I am. You being sexually active with just one girl is definitely a relief. Gianna's good for you. Other than a few calls from your school about ditching, you've been surprisingly well behaved."

I didn't know whether to laugh or hang up on her. "I'm hurt, aren't I still your good little boy?"

"I wish." Her tone was laced with humor. "But at least I haven't had to pick you up at the police station lately."

"I was always framed," I assured her, striving for a sincere tone.

"Caleb, I'll never believe someone mistook you for a valet outside that restaurant and that's why you and Dante went for a joyride in a one-hundred thousand dollar sports car or that someone spiked your drink at a party and that's why you got arrested for underage drinking when you were *thirteen*."

I knew she was making light of all the trouble I'd caused, purposely ignoring the worst of my transgressions.

And I loved her for it.

She hated talking about when I got arrested for putting a guy in the hospital, landing me in juvenile hall for a few days and on probation afterwards. I'd never regret it, though. If I saw a guy hurting a woman, then I'd be the one hurt him. I did it back then when Claudette's ex showed up at her apartment to beat her. I did it again when Josh repeatedly hurt Gianna.

The fact that Claudette, my older upstairs neighbor at my mom's place, and I were only in a casual relationship didn't matter. I would do the same for any female. Being on probation was what held me back from hurting Josh even worse than I had.

The asshole got off lucky.

Back to the present, I told my mom, "I'm sorry for being such a pain in the past. Things are different now. I have a reason to be good."

I could hear the smile in her voice. "Gianna?"

"Yes," I agreed, grinning like a fool.

"Has her mom come around?"

My grin disappeared. "No, she's still being stubborn."

"What are you guys going to do?"

"Whatever we have to, see each other secretly for now."

"Why your father married that woman, I'll never understand."

I pitied my dad, but I wasn't sure I understood either. "He loved her, I guess. I think he still does."

"Well, at least one thing came out of it, you met Gianna and now I can sleep at night without worrying what kind of trouble you're getting into."

My mind wandered to what kind of things I'd like to be doing at night with Gianna.

My mom interrupted my thoughts, "So you love her?"

"Yes." The stupid grin was back. "I'm keeping her."

"I'm happy for you, honey."

"Thanks, mom. I'm happy for me too."

"You're welcome to bring her here anytime."

"Thanks. I just got to dad's. I'll call you tomorrow."

"Bye, honey." She hung up and I threw my phone into the cup holder.

When I got home I'd fill my dad in on the situation between Gianna and me and hope I'd have his support also.

GIANNA

"Gianna, who dropped you off earlier?" my mom asked, her voice filled with distrust.

As soon as I was through the front door earlier, I'd run up the stairs to my room. Now, I was sitting and eating dinner at the dining room table with my mom and Chance. This was the room I'd first met Caleb in. I stifled a sigh and tried to hide how happy I was. I might not have been doing a very good job, which had brought out my mom's easily suspicious nature.

Trying to act casual, I brought down the forkful of spaghetti I'd been about to eat. "My friend, Ian."

My mom's eyes narrowed, not satisfied with my answer. "Tell me about him."

Not feeling one bit guilty about lying to my treacherous mother, I went right into it. "Let's see, he's really handsome and plays football at Denver West High School."

I had to hold back laughter at the thought of Ian as a jock. He was so not the type. I saw him more as the head of an illegal gambling ring, taking bets behind the gym on sporting games. Although, with his swanky upbringing, I wouldn't be surprised if he golfed or played tennis. I'd have to ask him. I rocked a tennis court.

My mom looked pleased, some of her earlier doubt gone. "Are you dating?"

I gnawed a chunk of my French bread off, trying to divert her attention. My mom hated it when I didn't eat ladylike. Chance copied me, grunting as he tore at a piece of bread with his teeth. I gave him a wink.

"Gianna!" my mom snapped to get my attention.

My mouth full of bread, I answered truthfully, "We're not dating." I managed to hide my horror at the thought. I liked Ian as a friend, but now the thought of being with anyone but Caleb made me want to shudder, and not in the good way Caleb made me do it.

"Gianna, don't talk with food in your mouth," she scolded.

I took another bite of spaghetti. "Well, stop bugging me when I'm eating."

Okay, lying to my mom was actually something I was enjoying. My own little revenge for all the hurt and hassle she'd put me and Caleb through.

"Is his family rich?" I hated when she asked questions like that, as if money was more important than character. I'd always suspected the main reason she let me spend so much time on the weekends with Cece was because her parents owned a restaurant and were in the process of expanding to a second location. They weren't millionaires, but they'd totally renovated a modest home in Cherry Creek.

I gave her a fake smile, one I'd first learned in all those stupid pageants and had perfected while in high school. "Very rich, you'd totally approve." She was making me angry and I couldn't help adding, "I think his dad is single. Want me to hook you up? He could be husband number three."

"That was uncalled for, Gianna," my mom chided.

Whatever, I wasn't the one who'd driven away one husband and threw away another perfectly good one, no, a *great* one. At this rate, she'd be on a fourth husband by the time she was forty. She was so narrow-minded she didn't realize how stupid she was being. She might be fairly young and attractive still, but she wouldn't be both of those forever. Scott had loved her and there was no guarantee she'd find another like him.

She frowned. "But you still spend the night at Cece's house, right?"

"Yep," I answered, wanting to change the subject. "So, Chance, how was school today?"

"Fine," he mumbled then took a drink of his milk. He had spaghetti sauce on one cheek and I wiped it with a napkin for him. He moved his head away as if I were harassing him. He'd been quiet since Scott left and it was just another reason for me be pissed at my mom. How many dads was he going to lose because she was a dumb bitch?

"This Ian sounds like a good catch," she commented.

Having a mother who encouraged me to be a gold digger was sickening. "Maybe I'll date him so I can get knocked up by a rich guy like you did."

It was true. The child support my dad paid was more than the average adult's salary. And even when they first got together in their teens, I don't think it was a coincidence that she'd dated a guy who came from money.

She was momentarily shocked but then surprised me by reaching over to slap my face. Cheek stinging, my eyes immediately went to Chance, who now looked like he was about to cry. I felt guilt about my part in the upheaval in his life. Since he was five, he'd known a stable home with a good stepdad. Now he had to deal with a divorce and a family in turmoil.

I glared at my mom. "Do you have to act like a psycho in front of my little brother?"

She returned my look, not about to admit she'd ever done anything wrong. "Go to your room."

Jumping out of my chair, it toppled back to hit the floor. "I'm calling dad!"

Her face went white, knowing he'd chew her ass out for hitting me. "Gianna!" she yelled after me as I ran up the stairs. I wasn't about to let her talk me out of it. Slamming my bedroom door, I made sure to lock it.

My dad didn't answer his cell so I tried his home phone. He must have checked the caller id, because he answered with, "Gianna?"

Riled up, I rushed to say, "Why did you have to breed with a crazy person? I mean, wasn't there anyone better to choose from in the mental hospital?"

My dad, always ready to listen to me vent about my mom, laughed. "What has she done now? I've told you before, you're always welcome to move here and live with me in Houston."

I scowled. "Are you still dating that bimbo?"

"Mia's a surgeon and hardly a bimbo. But no, we aren't together anymore. She's still a good friend."

"I still think she slept her way through medical school *and* she has fake breasts."

I was glad they weren't dating anymore. When we would visit my dad, Mia would suck up to me and Chance in front of him, but when he wasn't around, she'd act like we didn't exist. She was never outright mean, but it used to confuse the heck out of my little brother. Good stepmother material, she was not.

I sighed sadly, thinking how much easier life would be if I lived with him. "Dad, can't you move back to Denver?"

He groaned. "You're making me feel like a terrible father, Gianna."

"You're an awesome dad. You just have poor taste in women." In a softer voice, I said, "Chance and I need you."

"I'll think about it," he promised, not sounding too sure. "We'll see."

"That's all I ask. Just think about it." I decided to play dirty. "With mom divorcing Scott, Chance won't have a man in his life."

I realized it was a deliberate change of subject on his part when he asked, "Your mom mentioned something about Scott's stepson."

Startled, I wondered just how much she'd told my dad. Generally, they didn't get along, but every once in a while they'd have a real conversation.

"Yeah?" I prompted, trying to sound innocent.

"That you were seeing him?"

"Uh-huh," I responded vaguely.

"That she didn't approve?" Unfortunately, my dad was going for the same vague approach.

"Overreaction on her part," I assured him. "You would have liked him, dad." That was probably a lie. Caleb was a father's worst nightmare. Well, maybe not worst since there were guys way worse than him.

"Are you still seeing him?" Unlike my mother, I hated lying to my dad.

"I want to," I hedged, afraid he'd tell my mom if I confided in him.

In a tired voice, he said, "Just be honest with me, Gianna. I'd rather you tell me the truth."

"You won't tell mom?"

"I won't tell your mother."

"I love him."

My dad, just a year older than my mom, was still youthful in personality. Not like the woman downstairs who was only thirty-three but acted like she's fifty-three. I knew he'd understand where I was coming from.

"Just be careful," he advised with evident worry. Unlike my mom, my dad was more able to treat me like an equal. He would never try to order me around like she did, but he would want to help me make smart decisions.

"Don't worry, dad, he loves me too."

"I've got another call coming in, sweetie. Have Chance call me later?"

"Sure, and you'll think about moving back here? There are plenty of people who need nose jobs and tummy tucks here in Denver." As a plastic surgeon, I imagined it wouldn't be simple for my dad to move here, but after a lot of effort it'd be worth it.

"I promise I'll think about it."

After getting off the phone with him, I flopped down onto my bed and turned on the television. I hadn't told my dad about my mom smacking me because I didn't want to make the situation worse than it was.

Ignoring the reality show on TV, I thought about my cute boyfriend. It was so amazing being back together. He'd changed so much from the guy he used to be. I trusted him not to hurt me. Even if I couldn't claim him publicly, he was mine. He'd said the most romantic things today. Well, romantic for him and in between saying lots of naughty things. Not that I minded the naughty stuff.

I was anxious to see him at school tomorrow. Maybe we'd ditch and sneak off somewhere together.

Reluctantly, I pulled out of my backpack the book I was supposed to be reading for English. Our teacher had let us pick between Slaughterhouse-Five and The Scarlet Letter. My class had chosen Slaughterhouse-Five and the way the plot jumped around it was like a Quentin Tarantino movie. It was interesting, but I wished it had more romance in it.

I started to drift off to sleep while reading, but shot up when my phone beeped a text message alert. It was from Caleb.

Caleb: *Hey, beautiful, I'm going to sneak into your house tonight and bang you*

I slapped a hand over my mouth to muffle my laughter. Some things never changed. I'd better savor the few romantic words he'd said today and last night 'cause he still thought like a player most of the time.

But now he was a one-woman player.

CHAPTER FIFTEEN

*"Meeting you was fate, becoming your friend was a choice,
but falling in love with you was beyond my control."*
-Anonymous

CALEB

I'd never thought there'd be a day when receiving attention from
hot girls would be a chore, something undesirable.

As a cute brunette moved so close to me on the cafeteria bench
her breasts were brushing against my arm, I felt something hit the
back of my head. Twisting around to look down at the floor behind
me, I spotted a baby carrot. I glanced up to see Gianna giving me a
dirty look from one table over.

I gave her a helpless look and gesture. Rolling her eyes, she
turned her head away to listen to whatever some guy had to say to
her. Kevin, I thought his name was. Why the hell did he have to talk
to her with his head so close? Did he just glance down at her chest?

I wasn't sure I'd make it through a year and a half of this crap.
Bending down, I picked up the baby carrot and chucked it at the guy
talking to her.

Bullseye.

It thumped him right on the forehead. His eyes shot to mine,
looking pissed, until he noticed my killing look. His face blanched
and he must've got the message because he jumped up out of his seat
in the pretense of taking his tray to the trash.

Gianna's giggle improved my mood.

Maybe I should join a sport, I had good aim. Julie would approve
since in her unstable mind, wearing a jock strap equaled being good
enough to date her daughter.

Moving my eyes down the table where Gianna sat, I saw Josh
sitting at the end, watching our exchange. I flipped him off and
turned back around.

This entire situation sucked. Last night that hateful woman, Julie,
showed up at my dad's condo and tried to reconcile with him. She
must have realized what an idiot she'd been to lose a devoted
husband.

I'd been in my room upstairs at the time, but cracked my bedroom door open to listen to what was going on down there between her and my dad. Whatever happened between them directly affected me and Gianna. I was a concerned party.

Plus, I'd been primed to go down there and protect him from her viciousness if I had to.

Instead, as I'd listened to her words, they were sugary sweet and mildly seductive. She'd been telling my dad how much she loved and missed him. How she just wanted things the way they were before. That they could be happy again and a divorce wasn't necessary.

Unfortunately, my dad had sounded like he was falling for it. Until Julie mentioned it would be better off for everyone if I moved back in with my mom. That was when my dad had exploded in anger. I'd been so proud of him. Did she really think she could come over and manipulate him into seeing things her way?

The grin on my face was likely maniacal as I'd listened to him tell her off. He'd told her if she couldn't accept me, then he wanted to go forward with the divorce. That was when her true crazy-ass colors had emerged and she'd started yelling about what a loser I was.

The words she spewed were offensive but my feelings weren't hurt. No parent liked anyone badmouthing their kid, so I could imagine the look on my dad's face.

She'd ended her tirade with threats if I ever came near her daughter again. How little she knew. I planned on coming near and *inside* her daughter as much as possible. She was just too stupid to realize that Gianna no longer belonged to her.

Unable to shut her up, my dad had yelled for her to leave and seconds later the front door was slamming shut. I'd quietly closed my bedroom door to give my dad some privacy. He'd done what he had to do as a man, but it'd probably still hurt him to do it. For some unexplainable reason, he loved Julie.

I was so lost in remembering the night before, I almost didn't notice when Gianna walked past my table on her way out of the cafeteria.

Was the shake in that cute ass for me?

I was curious enough to send Gianna a text asking her.

She texted back: *I'm surprised you even noticed me, with all those girls hanging on you*

I smiled at her jealousy. What had been a turnoff in other girls was adorable in her.

I texted back: *What girls? There's only one girl in my world and that's you*

She sent back: *Aw, I love you. Meet me at your car in two minutes?*

Brushing off the girl who was hanging onto my arm, I tossed the rest of my lunch in the trash before leaving the cafeteria. I was contemplating how to convince Gianna to skip the rest of our classes with me as I walked out of the school and through the parking lot. Maybe we'd take a drive to the nearest park. That always worked well for us.

When I reached my car, Gianna was leaning against it, a naughty smile on her face. That was one of my favorite Gianna smiles. That smile usually meant good things for me. It was too bad I'd been so stubborn three years ago about meeting my stepfamily. I could've been on the receiving end of that smile years ago.

*****

For the rest of the school week, things pretty much went the same. We resisted ditching as much as possible, but didn't resist the temptation entirely. On Tuesday morning, we went out to breakfast, but made it to school in time for third period. We took the entire day off on Thursday and went to Elitch Gardens amusement park before it closed for the upcoming winter. Gianna told her mom she was going with some of the cheerleaders.

Often I stared at her while we were in school. I felt better whenever she was near, like during the two classes we had together and at lunch. She'd be annoyed if she knew how vulnerable I saw her when I wasn't around. When I was with her was the only time I could assure myself she was safe and happy.

We pretended we weren't on speaking terms, but our eyes spoke to each other plenty. Sometimes they conveyed words of love, but a lot of the time it was pure lust. I couldn't get enough of her and by her responses I figured it was the same for her. With a look she'd tell me how much she missed me or needed me.

Now it was Friday night and the football game was about to start. It was the last game of the season and my last chance until next year to see Gianna in her hot little cheerleader uniform. She was late meeting the other girls on the field because I'd talked her into the backseat of my car. We were parked at the far end of the lot where it was darkest.

She giggled as my hand crept up her thigh and under her skirt. I wanted to hear her moan. I liked the idea of her being out there cheering after I made her come. "Caleb, behave, I have to get to the game!"

"Shh," I told her. "It doesn't start for five minutes."

She made a disbelieving sound. "Since when do you only take five minutes?"

"So true," I muttered against her neck.

The next instant, I landed on the floor of the backseat with a thud. One thing bad about dating a girl who was a dancer was that her legs were damn strong. When I got back up on the seat, Gianna was sitting against the door straightening her clothing.

I sighed loudly in resignation. "Fine, I'll wait until after the game, but I'll have you know that watching you jump up and down out there is going to be torture."

She laughed, opening the door to climb out of the car. I watched her walk away, loving the sway of her hips in that little skirt.

Deciding to distract myself with food, I got in line at the concession stand. I missed kickoff, but found a choice spot at the bottom of the bleachers, right in front of the cheerleaders. Digging into my nachos, I didn't pay attention when someone sat down next to me.

"She should wear that outfit every day."

I almost spit out my food. Swallowing it down, I glared at the fuckhead sitting next to me. "What the hell are you doing here?"

Ian gestured to the cheerleaders below us. "I'm here to support Gianna in her extracurricular activities."

"Oh really," I bit out sarcastically. "Well, you can just go back home because I'm all the support Gianna needs."

He pointed at Gianna, who was watching our exchange with a curious look on her face. "She's already seen me. It'd probably hurt her feelings for me to leave so soon."

"I doubt it," I muttered. "Why are you bothering me? Find somewhere else to sit."

He shrugged. "Besides Gianna, you're the only person I know here." He turned his sly grin on me. "Plus, I knew it'd annoy you."

Tossing my food into a nearby trash can, I was reluctant to change seats. "I've lost my appetite."

In an indulgent voice he asked me, "Have you ever seen anything more adorable than Gianna shaking pom-poms?"

In response, I ignored him.

"So, which of the cheerleaders have you screwed, Caleb?" Ian leaned over to ask in a conspiratorial whisper.

I turned my head to give him a dirty look. "Only Gianna."

He scowled for a moment before wiping the look off his face and bumping his shoulder against mine as if we were buds. "Come on, you can tell me. I won't tell Gianna. Who have you messed around with? The brunette with the big tits?"

"Do you think I'm an idiot? First off, I'd never cheat on Gianna. Second, if I were stupid enough to do so, I definitely wouldn't tell my biggest rival."

His face transformed into satisfaction. "So, you admit I'm competition?"

"Not. Even. Close." Why was I letting him aggravate me? Rationally, I knew I had nothing to worry about. I'd already won the girl and her heart.

He scowled, not liking my confidence.

I grinned wide.

Scanning the field, he changed the subject, "So which number is her ex-boyfriend Josh?"

I looked at him out of the corner of my eye. "She told you about him?"

"Yep. If I get bored, I might kick his ass tonight."

"Already took care of it and I have no idea what his jersey number is." Though, it wouldn't be hard to find out.

"What about that Seth guy?"

He was trying to act nonchalant, but I sensed seriousness in him. Just how much did he like my girlfriend? Maybe he wasn't pretending to be interested in her to piss me off. I'd prefer it if his motivation was to annoy me. I didn't want him liking her for real. Hating the thought of another guy wanting a relationship with her, I wondered how I could get Ian out of her life.

"Don't know Seth's number either," I carefully explained. "Why do you care?"

His eyes didn't leave the game. "Just wondering."

Uh-huh. Sure.

Picking a plan, I asked him, "Do you want me to hook you up with one of the cheerleaders?"

He rolled his eyes at me derisively. "No thanks, you have crappy taste in chicks. Other than Gianna, you usually go for the dirty skanks."

"Before Gianna my taste in chicks was hot and easy. No different than you. When have you ever had a problem with that? Don't forget we've messed with some of the same girls." Saying it out loud made it sound skeezy. I shook off the memories with a shudder.

He laughed with genuine humor. "It was always fun stealing your dates."

I raised my eyebrows at him. "I had just as much fun stealing yours."

We grinned at each other and I got this weird feeling we were bonding or something lame like that. Turning my head away, I coughed into my fist.

Awkward.

For the remainder of the game, we didn't talk much, but instead watched the players and one cheerleader in particular. Although, I saw Ian's eyes stray to a couple other ones from time to time. Maybe he wasn't falling for my girlfriend after all. I'd ignore his taunts and see if I could get Gianna to hook him up with one of the girls. He *had* pointed out the brunette.

GIANNA

When was this freaking game going to end? It was torture having my man in the stands and unable to go near him. I'd tell my mom I was going to a party thrown by one of the football players and instead spend time with Caleb tonight. 'Cause in her mind kegs and wild parties were much more acceptable than being with the guy I loved.

As much as I would have preferred not to hide our relationship, it hadn't been so bad. Caleb and I had managed to spend quite a bit of time together this week. And it hadn't been all about sex, either. Sometimes we just held hands and cuddled, like when we went to the amusement park yesterday. Afterwards, we went to the Rocky Mountain Diner for dinner.

Ian had turned out to be a really good friend. He'd even come to watch me cheer tonight. I waved towards where he and Caleb were sitting together. They were actually talking to each other without throwing any punches, so maybe there was hope they'd become friends one day.

At the end of half-time, one of the other cheerleaders had handed me a piece of paper. I'd opened it to find a note from Caleb. It said in sloppy boy scrawl: *Meet me in the cafeteria after the game, love Caleb.*

So romantic and so naughty. But that was my boyfriend. He wanted to meet in the cafeteria probably for some naughty reason. I knew he liked to rebel against authority and school, but having sex in the cafeteria was just bad. Of course, I'd meet him anyways.

By the time the game ended we'd won by eight points. I was bouncing around like I had to go pee. I didn't, but I was antsy to be back in my boyfriend's arms. First, I went with the other girls to the locker room to grab my duffel bag.

Outside the locker room, I had my phone in my hand to text Caleb when I ran into Seth.

"Hey, Gianna, how's it going?" He was obviously headed for the boys' locker room, sweaty and carrying his helmet under one arm.

"It's going good, Seth. How about you?"

It was nice that he seemed to be taking the breakup much better. Tilting his head back, he grinned. "Got a date tonight."

"Nice," I drawled in approval. "See you later."

"Yeah," he replied, disappearing into the locker room.

My phone rang. Looking at the screen, I answered it while heading in the direction of the cafeteria. "Sup?"

"I am so mad at Dante right now," Cece informed me.

That could mean anything with Cece. "What happened?"

"We were supposed to go to the movies tonight but he cancelled to hang out with his friends."

"Which movie?" I asked, knowing Cece's horrible taste in films.

"That new Emma Stone one," she replied, confirming my guess.

I left the gym, cutting across the dark school grounds to the main building. "Well, there you go. It probably wasn't you he didn't want to see tonight, but the chick flick you were trying to make him go to."

"You think?"

"I know," I assured her.

Standing outside the doors to the cafeteria, I told her, "I gotta go. Call you later?"

"Sure, but I'm still mad at Dante. We always go to movies he picks. Sometimes I should be able to pick the movie, too."

"I totally agree. Bye, Cece."

"Later, Gigi."

I pressed the end button and dropped my phone into my bag. Yanking open the heavy cafeteria door, I walked into the large, dark room calling Caleb's name.

Huh, I thought I'd beat him here.

When an arm wrapped around my waist from behind, I jumped automatically then relaxed back into Caleb's chest. "I missed you."

He pressed his face into my hair and inhaled. "I've missed you too, Gianna."

That was when I realized it wasn't Caleb holding me.

I immediately started struggling in Josh's grip.

Until he flung me against a wall.

CHAPTER SIXTEEN

"I have decided to stick with love.
Hate is too great a burden to bear."
-Martin Luther King, Jr.

GIANNA

As I hit the wall, thankfully my head didn't bang against the concrete. But my back took quite a hit. I landed on the cafeteria floor, but was panicked enough to get myself in a sitting position within seconds. My eyes were squeezed shut in pain until a light shined on my face. Squinting them open, I tried to see past the glare of the flashlight shining on my face. I scrambled to my feet as the light moved steadily closer.

Putting on a brave front, I asked, "Hey, Josh, what do you want?"

"You."

Well, that didn't sound good.

"Listen," *–psycho–* "Josh, I really can't hang out with you right now. I'm supposed to be meeting the girls in the parking lot." Thinking quickly, I added, "Do you want to walk me there?"

"No."

Crap.

When he was just inches away with the flashlight now pointed down, I could make out his face in the soft glow. How did I ever find him attractive? All I saw now was his ugly personality.

I tried a different approach. "Whatever you think is going to happen, Josh, you're delusional."

"Am I?"

Well, *duh.*

Okay, enough of this. I very calmly turned to walk away and get the hell out of there. Grabbing my arm roughly, he effectively stopped me. Not wanting to show my rising fear, I tried to yank my arm away. "Let me go."

He shook his head. "No, that was my mistake before, letting you go."

Now I was starting to get annoyed. "You didn't have a choice."

"It's all *his* fault," Josh said in a distracted tone.

Danger! Bad Boy

140

I didn't have to ask who he meant.

Caleb.

He'd be wondering where I was right about now. The original plan had been to meet out in the parking lot after the game. Unfortunately, I'd been stupid enough to fall for that fake note and ended up in the empty cafeteria with my psycho ex-boyfriend.

Tired of playing this game, I used my free arm to try pushing away from him. He stumbled backwards a couple of steps, losing his grip on me, and I spun around to sprint towards the exit.

Not fast enough, though, because within three seconds he'd tackled me to the ground. We landed gracelessly on the cold linoleum, his arms wrapped around me from behind and me facedown against the floor.

"Get off me!" I screamed at the top of my lungs, hoping someone would hear.

"Shut, up!"

Wasn't there supposed to be a janitor here late at night? A dedicated teacher who practically lived here? Not about to give up on that idea, I screamed, "Help!" before Josh had the chance to clap a hand over my mouth.

Which I promptly bit.

He yelped in pain, yanking the meat of his hand out from between my teeth and using the same hand to grab me by the hair. Now I was really getting freaked. I started fumbling for the phone in the bag I still had over one shoulder. Pulling it out, I unlocked the screen, frantically trying to redial my last call.

"Give me that," Josh snarled, ripping the phone out of my hand and throwing it against the nearest wall. The sound of plastic cracking was discouraging. I doubted it even rang long enough for someone to pick up the other line.

Using his grip on my hair and around my waist, he slowly turned me over. The dropped flashlight was still rolling back and forth a couple feet away from the scuffle. As it slowed down, I could see the demented smile on Josh's face. A school psychologist would've been real handy right about now. And a taser gun. Unfortunately, my mace was on my dresser at home.

"Just say what you have to say, Josh. I need to get going. My mom is expecting me home soon," I bluffed.

His grip on my hair tightened, causing pain to shoot to my scalp. "Liar. You're meeting up with your stepbrother. The one you dumped me for."

"I didn't-" I began, only to be cut off when he started shaking me.

"Shut up!" he yelled. "I'll win you back. I'll show you how much I love you."

When he started fumbling around at the waist of his football pants, I realized his intentions.

Hell, freaking, no.

With his grip on my hair and his weight on me, I couldn't manage to get away, but my arms were free. I started hitting and punching him wherever I could, with no real skill, but with the determination of a girl who refused to be violated by some bastard who couldn't take *no* for an answer.

"Stop! Stop!" he demanded, jerking me around.

When I didn't stop, he grabbed onto one of my hands and bent it backwards. Trying to ignore the building pain in my wrist, I kept hitting him with my free hand. He was now straddling my waist, but using what strength I had in my legs, I tried to lift my hips and buck him off me.

The creep was heavy.

I swung my fist at his face. He dodged my wild punch and bent my hand back farther. The shock of hearing one or more bones in my wrist breaking temporarily ended my struggles. Tears streamed out of my eyes as I cradled my broken wrist with my unharmed hand. The searing pain was intense.

I gasped out, "Please let me up!"

Josh only got angrier. "Look what you made me do! I didn't want to hurt you!"

Could have fooled me.

He was still laying on me and my renewed struggles weren't nearly as energetic as before. God, it hurt. I'd never broken a bone in my life. I hadn't imagined how badly it would hurt.

"Please, Josh, I need to go to a hospital." Trying to think through the pain, I asked, "Will you drive me?"

He was quiet for a moment and I hoped this craziness was about to end. But then he said, "Not yet. Later. When you love me back."

142

So . . . never? Maybe I could fake it. "I do love you, Josh. I always have." Despite the tears and pain, I thought it sounded pretty convincing.

Josh groaned, smashing his lips against mine. Guess he bought it. I forced myself to kiss him back before turning my face to the side and whimpering, "It hurts so bad."

No faking there.

"Can we please go now, Josh?"

But it was as if he hadn't even heard me because he was fumbling with his pants again. In his messed up head, he thought I'd want to have sex with him, broken wrist and all.

As he reared back onto his knees to unzip, I took my chance and brought one of my own knees up into his crotch. I kneed him with a force that had him bent over in pain. He groaned, cupping himself. I scooted away from him on my back and managed to get up off the ground.

I heard, "Bitch!" right before a hand grabbed my shoulder and threw me back onto the ground.

The back of my head smacked against the hard surface, making me dizzy. Thankfully, my wrist hadn't taken any impact. When the momentary dizziness faded, I saw a fist flying towards my face at the same time I heard him yell, "You lied!"

His fist met my cheek and pain radiated over my face. I was lucky the blow hadn't knocked me out. I wasn't so lucky the second time when he punched my jaw as I felt excruciating pain and passed out.

I was unsure how long I'd been out but when I woke up, I realized two things. Josh was still there with me, hovering menacingly, and I was pretty sure he'd broken my jaw. I tasted blood in my mouth and my vision was still fuzzy.

Trying not to cry, because I needed to focus on the situation, I figured my best chance at that point was to pretend to be incapacitated. It probably wasn't far from the truth. I closed my eyes, pretending to pass out again.

A foot nudged my hip. "Quit faking, Gianna. I know you're awake."

From behind my closed lids, I could tell when he shone the flashlight on my face. I opened my eyes, but couldn't see his face with the bright light shining on mine. I tried moving my mouth to say something, but the pain prevented speech.

"Fucking, *fucking* bitch." He moved to stand over me, straddling my calves. Crouching down to sit on me, he said in a strange voice, "You know what your problem is, Gianna?"

Helpless, I laid there unmoving.

"You're a cold bitch. I bet you never even gave it up to Caleb, huh?" He barked out a laugh. "Well, let's find out."

I was confused about his meaning at first, but soon came to understand. Despite broken bones, I struggled as hard as before.

Maybe harder.

When he broke my other wrist for hitting him again, I barely felt the new pain. It simply blended in with everything else that was hurting.

When he started violating me with the large metal flashlight, I kicked out my legs, screaming through my clenched teeth. Never did I give up or give in to his abuse.

Until my vision went fuzzy and I finally passed out for good.

In the last seconds of consciousness, I prayed I wouldn't wake up again.

CALEB

"Really, you don't have to wait around. I can tell Gianna you said hello," I told Ian while giving him another look of disdain.

I was the boyfriend, not him. It was my job to wait around for Gianna after a game, not him. She wanted only me waiting for her, not him. Ian smiled, knowing how much his presence was irritating me. Deciding to try another tactic, I ignored him.

He refused to ignore me back. "What do you think is taking her so long? My guess is we've already seen all the other cheerleaders leave."

Ian was right. Most, if not all, of the other cheerleaders had passed us in the parking lot on the way to their vehicles. Where the hell was she? Starting to feel anxious, I told Ian, "I'm going to go look for her. Maybe she thought we were supposed to meet somewhere else."

I went walking off in the direction of the locker rooms.

"I'll go with you," Ian said casually, coming into step next to me. Of course he would. There was no getting rid of him.

We circled around the gym, yelled Gianna's name through the girl's locker room doors and checked the parking lot again, texting and calling her phone the entire time. No luck. Her phone was going straight to voicemail and she was nowhere in sight.

At that point, the place was starting to look deserted. Her Jeep was still in the parking lot, so she had to be around somewhere. Glancing sideways at Ian as we walked behind the bleachers, I tried to keep my cool.

"Uh, maybe she ran into the school to get something from her locker."

He was looking pretty worried himself. As the panic built in me, I was strangely relieved he was here. Then again, just looking at him still annoyed the crap out of me.

We checked one of the back entrances to the main building, but the doors were locked. Usually on game nights some entrance was left unlocked, with so many students, parents and teachers still on campus on Friday nights.

As we rounded the corner of the building, someone ran into me. The dude pushed me away from him. I braced myself for a fight. "Hey, what the fuck's your problem, man?"

His hoarse voice replied, "Just get out of my way."

The guy edged around me and a light posted high on the brick wall illuminated his face. Out of instinct, I was on him in seconds, grabbing him by the front of his jersey. "What are you still doing here, Josh?"

Josh was visibly shaken, his eyes looked wild, and it suddenly hit me. I slammed him against the side of the building. "Where the fuck is she?"

"God dammit," I heard Ian mutter. With everything Gianna had told him, Ian had come to the same conclusion as me. Gianna was nowhere to be found and we'd just stumbled upon Josh.

Josh tried to push me away from him, but my grip on his jersey and my forearms pressing against him managed to keep in place. Ian stepped up beside us and got in Josh's face. "Answer him, asshole. Where the fuck is Gianna?"

After a moment and no answer, Ian pulled back his arm and punched Josh in the ear. Josh's head whipped to the side. Thinking Ian had the right idea, I punched him in the gut.

He grunted in pain, cursing. Almost in a whisper, he said, "She got what she deserved."

This time, it was my fist flying at his face. I was trying to think straight and not panic, because flashing through my mind was the time I caught Josh banging Gianna against a wall. Clenching my teeth, I asked Josh again, "Where?"

He must've realized how totally screwed he was and after a few moment's hesitation, he spat out, "Cafeteria."

Not letting go of his shirt, I dragged him in that direction, with Ian right on our heels. Josh let out a desperate sound. "I told you where she is, let me go. I have things to do."

I didn't bother responding. When the double doors came in sight, Ian jogged forward and opened one. Pushing Josh inside ahead of me, he stumbled. "She's not here," I said automatically when we entered the dark room.

Josh turned around and made to leave. "She must have left." Raising my arms, I pushed Josh a few feet back into the room.

Ian mumbled, "Where the hell are the lights?" right before the cafeteria was flooded in light.

It took a second or two for our eyes to adjust to the brightness. At my first good look at Josh, dread settled in my stomach. There was a small amount of blood smeared on the white material of his football pants.

He held up his hands in a placating gesture and I lost it when I saw the blood on the palm of his right hand. My eyes darted frantically around the cafeteria until they landed on the person lying on the floor about thirty feet away in a cheerleader uniform. At the same time I spotted her, Ian was already running towards her, calling out her name. She didn't respond.

I shouted, "Call 911!" to Ian at the same time I lunged for Josh.

The next ten minutes were an unthinking haze of rage. The cops showed up first, one of them pulling me off Josh as his female partner leaned over Gianna's lifeless figure. When the cop yanked me off Josh, he merely opened the way for Ian to take his turn. The sense of satisfaction that coursed through me as Ian slammed a metal folding chair into Josh and I heard the sound of ribs breaking did nothing to dull the rage.

At that point, the paramedics showed up with a gurney. The cop let go of me to tackle Ian and I ran to Gianna, praying silently. The paramedics demanded I stay out of their way, but I saw what was done to her.

It'd be burned in my memory forever.

The left side of her face was swollen and I overheard the paramedics I was hovering over caution each other to be careful of her broken wrists. I glanced over to where Ian was yelling and saw the male cop handcuffing him after pinning Ian onto his stomach on the floor.

My gaze went back down to Gianna and I wanted so badly to pick her up, cradle her, but I knew I had to let them do their job. I didn't know what to do. There was nothing I *could* do. My eyes were wet with helpless tears.

When the female cop stepped in front of me with a pair of handcuffs and said, "I'm going to have to take you in," I simply nodded my head absently. As she placed the handcuffs on me, a second set of paramedics showed up and began administering to Josh.

The female cop must have called for another ambulance while I was being pulled off Josh. I wanted to scream at them to leave him there to rot. He didn't deserve any help. He deserved handcuffs or a fucking bullet to the head.

More cops arrived and they sat Ian and me with our backs against a nearby wall. Ian answered the questions asked because I couldn't be bothered. My eyes were glued to Gianna.

My girl was hurt and I couldn't do one fucking thing to make it better. I hadn't protected her. I hadn't been on time to save her.

When one of the cops dropped a bloody flashlight into an evidence bag, I wanted to scream.

As they wheeled Gianna on the gurney out of the cafeteria and I couldn't follow, I did scream.

CHAPTER SEVENTEEN

*"There is always some madness in love. But there
is also always some reason in madness."*
-Friedrich Nietzsche

CALEB

"I should have hit him in the head with that chair," Ian mused for the hundredth time.

"Shut the hell up," I mumbled, keeping my forearm over my eyes as I lay on the bunk. I might be forced to share a cell with him, but that didn't mean I had to look at his ugly mug.

"How many ribs do you think I broke, C?" Ian asked, pretending to be oblivious to my need for solitude.

"Do not nickname me. We are so not on a nickname basis," I ground out between clenched teeth.

Somehow I'd wound up in hell. Had I missed the part where I died? Who'd decided it would be a good idea to throw us in a cell together? Last night, Ian and I had taken turns beating the crap out of Josh. What made the cops think we wouldn't turn on each other? I'd imagined punching Ian in the face many times since we landed in here. Knowing us though, if we started fighting, we wouldn't stop until we were out of here, or they separated us.

After the paramedics had taken Gianna and Josh to the hospital, the cops took me and Ian to the police station. They'd grilled us separately for hours, making us tell our story over and over. My dad had showed up with a lawyer, the same one my parents used for me before. Only a lawyer had shown up for Ian.

When there wasn't a cop in my face, I was freaking out about Gianna.

I should've been more alert when it came to Josh. I should've known he wouldn't let it go and he'd do something extreme. Looking back, the signs were there, but my head had been someplace else. Lost in Gianna, I'd stopped taking anything else seriously. Stupid mistake, and my beautiful girl had paid for it.

Before they were done interrogating us, I'd asked my dad to run down to the hospital and check on her. I'd also bitched to the cops until they finally let me know Josh had in fact been handcuffed to his bed at the hospital. I guess once they'd realized he was the one to brutalize her, it wouldn't be such a great idea to have him free in the same hospital as her.

My dad wasn't back by the time they'd moved us from the police station to the holding facility for juveniles. They were supposed to release us into our parents' custody once our parents showed up. For Ian that might be awhile, since he was pretty sure his dad was out of the country.

I wasn't worried about my dad showing up. My mom would have already been here, but she was in Phoenix again for an art show. If my dad hadn't come back from the hospital yet, it was for a good reason. I just prayed he came back with good news about Gianna.

I should've probably been grateful Ian hadn't shut his trap. Otherwise I'd probably be going crazier. I felt already as if I was on the edge. I wasn't satisfied with the beating Josh got. The things he'd done to her. . . .

Some broken ribs and a busted up face didn't even begin to cover what he deserved. He deserved to go to hell. Forget prison, straight to hell should be his destination.

I was also trying not to freak out about the fact I wasn't with Gianna right now. Sure, her mom was down at the hospital and her dad was probably on a plane right now from Houston. But she needed me. And I badly needed to see her.

I'd heard the paramedics listing off her injuries, so I knew none of them were life threatening, but she must be in severe pain. And not just physically. I didn't have any experience dealing with anyone who'd been sexually assaulted, but I could imagine the kind of comfort and patience she needed.

I'd do anything to make it better for her. It was tearing me apart, what she'd suffered. Desperation to get to her had me jumping up to pace the cell.

"Caleb Morrison," a deep voice said from outside the cell. Automatically, I spun around, eager to get out.

"Yeah?"

"Your dad's here to take you home," the guard informed me while unlocking the bars.

"Thank God," I let out on a breath.

I was slipping out of the cell before the guard had a chance to swing it open all the way. It closed behind me with a clank and I turned my head back to give Ian a pitying look. "Sorry, man."

He shrugged from where he lounged on the top bunk. "No worries, I'm sure my dad will show up sometime next week."

Feeling uncomfortable, I gave him a quick, "Later," and walked ahead of the guard down the corridor. As soon as I spotted my dad waiting for me, I was asking questions. "How is she? Has she asked for me? Is she awake?"

My dad seemed uneasy and wasn't looking me in the eye. "Caleb, we'll discuss this when we get home."

"I'm not going home! I'm going to the hospital!" I practically yelled at him as we exited the building.

He stopped me in the parking lot with a hand on my shoulder. "Julie has given instructions that you aren't allowed in Gianna's hospital room."

Shrugging off his hand, I walked faster to the car. "That's bullshit! Take me to pick up my car at the school and I'll drive there myself."

My dad settled behind the wheel, letting out a sigh. "Fine, I'll take you to the hospital, but don't expect to get into her room. Her dad, Chris, is already there and Julie has given him an earful."

Driving to the hospital, my dad filled me in on Gianna's condition. Casts on both wrists, jaw wired shut and stitches down below. It was too much to bear, but I had to know. When he was done, I turned my head to look out the window so my dad wouldn't see my wet eyes. Knowing I needed privacy at that moment, my dad gave me the silence I needed to digest it all.

The car came to a stop in the parking garage and I jumped out. I felt impatient as my dad got out and circled around the car. Not knowing her room number, I was forced to wait for him to take me to her.

"Caleb, she may not even be awake yet. They still had her sedated earlier this morning."

"It's been over twelve freaking hours since it happened and she's probably wondering where the hell I am!" I shouted at him, needing to take my pain and frustration out on someone.

Danger! Bad Boy

My dad pulled me in for a hug and I allowed it. Allowed him to try to soothe away some of the ugliness roiling inside me. But nothing could make me feel better. "How bad was it, dad?"

My dad let out a choking sound and I realized how hard this was on him too. I loved Gianna, but so did he. My dad had been her stepfather for the past three years. He pulled back from the hug, fighting for composure.

"They stitched her up, and there's swelling and bruising, but they think she'll heal completely." A sound escaped his lips, but he swallowed visibly, getting himself under control. "They think she'll still be able to have children. He only used the flashlight on her, so at least we don't have to worry about pregnancy. Sick little bastard." My dad stopped there, wiping at his eyes.

Feeling cold all over, I didn't know how to deal with what happened to her.

How did I even begin to help her?

"And Josh?"

"I wish I could say he'd died from his injuries," my dad muttered angrily. "He's got a broken nose, busted up face and three broken ribs." When he hesitated, I glanced at him, seeing his wry smile. "You and that other kid really worked him over."

"Which room number is Josh in?"

"Caleb," my dad said sternly.

I gave my dad a false smile which probably looked more like a sneer. "To send him flowers, of course."

He shook his head. "He's not here anymore."

"Prison hospital?" I asked hopefully.

"Uh, no. Gianna's dad, Chris, took a midnight flight here and after getting briefed by the police, he asked the same thing you just did." My dad gave me a pointed look. "The police and hospital staff thought it best Josh be moved to another hospital for both his sake and her family's."

"I'm going to kill him," I told him in all seriousness. My dad was stressed by my statement so I attempted to reassure him, "Don't worry, I won't get caught."

He shook his head again. "You're in enough trouble. Assaulting Josh while you're already on probation for assault wasn't the brightest idea."

"I think it was an excellent idea," I mumbled stubbornly. I still had a taste for more of Josh's blood. I'd busted up that face of his and Ian had broken some ribs, but he had a lot more coming to him. That twisted creep hadn't begun to experience the pain coming his way.

Leaving the hospital parking garage, the glass doors at the front hospital entrance were a short ways ahead. "One more thing, Caleb." I could tell what he had to say wouldn't be good. "The cops started questioning the other cheerleaders and football players today."

"And?"

"They found out Josh had one of the cheerleaders pass a note to Gianna," he hesitated before going on, "Supposedly from you, asking to meet in the cafeteria after the game."

"*Fuck!*" I screamed, scaring the crap out of an elderly couple coming off the elevator.

My dad apologized to them, but they hustled past us faster than people their age should be able to move.

Stepping into the elevator, my dad pushed the button for the sixth floor. My stomach was tied in knots. I needed to be able to see Gianna and was worried I'd be denied. I hoped Julie wasn't here now. I might be able to get past Gianna's dad. Fifth floor, sixth floor, the elevator slid open.

"Dad?"

"Yeah?"

"What will I be dealing with when it comes to Chris?" I asked, wishing to hear he wanted to pat me on the back for beating the shit out of Josh.

"Well," my dad paused, obviously thinking over his answer, "When Julie first called him last night, she was convinced you were the one who hurt Gianna."

"Stupid bitch," I growled vehemently.

My dad ignored me calling his wife a bitch. "But, by the time Chris got here and the cops filled him in, he was just grateful you and Ian found Gianna so quickly and she wasn't lying there all night."

The thought of that . . . *fuck.*

We walked past the nurse's triage desk and my dad came to a stop in front of room 626. Unfortunately, I could already make out Julie's grating voice inside. My dad went in ahead of me and I was close on his heels. The room wasn't large and the curtains were closed. Julie sat in one chair against the window and a man sat in another chair, with Chance sleeping in his lap. This was a bad time to be meeting Gianna's dad.

Julie didn't see me right away, looking at my dad first, but when she did, she jumped out of her chair pointing a finger at me in accusation. "I don't want you in here!"

Ignoring her, I stared at the figure in the bed. She was lying on her back in a hospital gown, with the sheets pulled up to under her armpits. Both wrists were in casts and her face was badly swollen.

From what my dad had told me, the fracture in her jaw wasn't as bad as it could have been. Doctors estimated it'd take six weeks to heal. The wires they'd used would prevent Gianna from eating solid foods and she wouldn't be able to talk much, but once healed, she'd be back to normal.

At least physically.

Her eyes were closed. She was either asleep or still sedated. I prayed she wasn't having bad dreams.

Glancing at Julie, I took in her face turning red, twisted in hatred. It was amazing how such a pretty woman could become so ugly in a matter of seconds. "Did you not hear me, Caleb? You're not welcome here! This is all *your* fault!"

Gianna's dad stood up, settling a sleeping Chance into the armchair. "Take this outside, Julie. The kids don't need to hear it."

Reluctantly agreeing with him and not wanting Gianna to wake up upset, I spun on my heel and left the room. My dad was right behind me for support, but I could also hear the click of Julie's heels. In the hallway, I spun around again, crossing my arms over my chest. I needed to keep myself in check because Julie was undoubtedly about to piss me the fuck off. I'd have to resist the urge to smack her.

"Take your son home, Scott," Julie told my dad, not even bothering to address me.

"I'm here to be with Gianna," I protested. "You don't own the hospital, Julie."

Chris came out of the room, leaning against the doorframe. He was younger than I'd expected, younger than my dad, but I sometimes forgot Chris and Julie had gotten pregnant with Gianna while they were still in high school.

Around mine and Gianna's age, actually.

The fact he'd managed to get through college to become a plastic surgeon was amazing. Chris wore a neutral expression, so I couldn't tell where he stood in this little drama. This had to be eating him up inside. His daughter had been viciously attacked and violated. None of us needed Julie's selfish behavior.

"But, I *am* her mother and I say who can and can't come into her hospital room. And you're not welcome in there." She shot a look at Chris. "Her dad will back me up on this."

Chris lost the blank expression, giving me an apologetic look. "I think it's for the best for now. Gianna doesn't need any added stress." Julie was the one causing a ruckus.

I could almost understand where he was coming from, but I didn't have to like it. Stubbornly, I took a seat in one of the connected plastic and metal chairs in the hallway. "Fine, then I'll wait here until it's okay for me to see her."

Julie huffed and made to go back into the room.

I called out after her, "But, you may want to take some of the blame yourself, Julie, since Gianna would've never been in that cafeteria if you hadn't forced us to sneak around behind your back!"

Not looking back, she shut the door to Gianna's room behind her.

Chris's eyes were tired and his face suddenly haggard. From the look on his face I figured he didn't like Julie much more than I did. He muttered something about going to the cafeteria to get something for Chance when he woke up then he was gone.

My dad waited with me all day, running downstairs to get us magazines and food. I felt like crap, having not showered or changed my clothes since yesterday. Finally after dark, my dad was able to talk me into going home to clean up. Two hours later, I'd showered, packed a bag, picked up my car at the school parking lot and was back at the hospital.

Nearing room 626, the door was halfway open so I peeked inside. Julie obviously took Chance home after I'd left, because it was just Gianna's dad in there, sleeping in the same chair Chance had earlier. The lights were off in the room, but the bathroom light was on, providing a soft glow.

I set my bag down inside the doorway and edged closer to the bed. Gianna was slightly turned to her side now, but at a couple feet away I was surprised to see her eyes were open. An involuntary sound escaped my lips and I quickly crouched down onto the floor beside the bed so we were face to face.

"Baby," I whispered, not wanting to wake Chris.

Her eyelids dropped, but I saw the shine of tears trickle down. "Shh," I awkwardly tried to soothe her. The tears fell faster, along with my own.

"Please look at me, Gianna," I encouraged her softly.

After a long moment she opened her eyes and the pain I witnessed in them made me want to scream and rage, tear something apart. I swallowed it down, kissing her on the forehead.

Holding her gaze, I asked, "You know I love you, right?"

Her head jerked in a little nod, but she averted her eyes again.

I touched her gently on the head, stroking her hair. "I'm so sorry this happened, but I'll do whatever it takes to help you through it. Whatever you need, baby."

She didn't move and I knew she couldn't respond properly with her jaw wired shut. The nurse came into the room to administer more painkillers through the IV. Lying, I told the nurse I was Gianna's cousin.

Her dad woke up while I was speaking to the nurse and gave me a look that let me know he wasn't happy with my methods, but wouldn't kick me out. I pulled up a chair next to Gianna's bed and settled in.

After administering the drugs, the nurse left and Gianna drifted off to sleep. I was simply grateful for the time I'd get with Gianna until Julie showed up in the morning. It soothed my own demons to be near her again. But it'd be a long time before any of us were completely healed.

CHAPTER EIGHTEEN

"Immature love says 'I love you because I need you.'
Mature love says 'I need you because I love you.'"
-Erich Fromm

CALEB

Frustration wasn't a feeling that was ever easy to deal with. Helplessness was often its companion. I understood where she was coming from, I really did. But I couldn't help feeling that I should've been with her right now. Didn't she need me as much as I needed her?

Gianna had texted that it was only temporary, just until her dad could close up shop in Houston and find a place in Denver. She hadn't even enrolled in school there, but was getting her assignments faxed from school here. Trying to squash the panicky feeling that she wouldn't be coming back at all was all I could do.

Spending time with my parents wasn't helping. Hanging out with friends wasn't helping either. Gianna back in Denver was the only thing that could make me feel better. It'd been two weeks since she was released from the hospital and the very same day she'd gotten on a plane with her dad and flown to Houston.

If I weren't so freaking miserable myself, I'd find twisted satisfaction in Julie's predicament. Her life had gone to shit like the rest of ours. My dad wouldn't take her back because she obviously wasn't going to change her stance on me. The divorce was moving forward.

Besides that problem, Julie had to deal with the wrath of Chris. While at the hospital, I'd overheard an entertaining conversation, well argument really, where Chris had laid into Julie and called her a bad mother. He'd also stated that she'd had her chance to raise their kids and obviously he needed to take over. I was all for his idea, but the man needed to bring my girl back.

Like *now*.

I wasn't sure where Gianna and I stood. If I texted her that I loved and missed her, she'd return the sentiments, but with her jaw wired shut, she couldn't talk well enough for us to converse over the phone. Our relationship had been reduced to a series of texts and emails.

I craved her, needed her with me again.

I needed things back the way they were before, Gianna a short drive away, us together whenever we had the chance. We talked about only the most superficial things in emails and even through text messages I could sense her distancing herself from me. With her being all the way in Houston and me stuck here, I had no way to fix it.

We hadn't talked about what had happened. I'd rather not do it over text messages or emails. The right time would be when she was in my arms again. In person, I'd be able to help her the way she needed. I trusted Chris was getting her the help she needed.

But I couldn't help feeling what she needed most was me.

I'd gotten suspended from school for beating the shit out of Josh. So I'd been doing my schoolwork from home also. The school was trying to decide what to do with me, whether or not to expel me. On the one hand, Josh had assaulted Gianna and my reaction had been provoked and totally justifiable. On the other hand, I'd beaten the shit out of him badly enough to land him in the hospital.

The bright side of all this was that Josh had already gotten expelled. He was also arrested the moment he'd been released from the hospital. My dad had kept in contact with Julie enough to let me know what was going on with the charges against Josh.

I cringed at the thought of my own upcoming meeting with the justice system. Next week I had to go in front of a juvenile court judge for assaulting Josh.

It probably wouldn't have been such a big deal, but I was already on probation for assault for when I'd beat up Claudette's ex-boyfriend the night he'd shown up at her apartment and hit her. I'd put him in the hospital just like Josh and my lawyer was afraid the pattern of behavior would look bad to the judge. At the time I'd been found guilty of assaulting the other guy, the judge had claimed I'd gone too far in my effort to protect Claudette, something about unnecessary force.

By that point, I'd already been arrested for minor offenses and the assault charge had called for major action on the justice system's part, hence probation. I'd visited my probation officer the other day and he hadn't been too happy with me. The guy was an ass.

Lying on my bed, listening to depressing music, feeling sorry for myself, I sent Gianna another text.

Miss you

After four minutes, I was watching the clock, I got a text back:

Miss you too

Okay, I'd take that.

Love you, beautiful

Love you too

Right, that made me feel marginally better.

Can't wait to hold you again, princess

I knew it was hard for her to text with her broken wrists, so I waited patiently. Ten minutes later her next text came.

Watching a movie with my dad

When are you coming home?

She sent back, *Not sure*

Have court next week

Three minutes later, *Hope you don't get in trouble because of me*

Not your fault, any of it

When she still hadn't messaged back fourteen minutes later, I texted her again.

How are you?

She finally texted me back.

Fine

That didn't tell me much. I gave up for now, frustrated by the lack of communication. When we were face-to-face again, I wouldn't let her hide from me.

I sent her, *Love you, TTYL*

Okay

The helpless, panicky feeling was back again. What the hell was I supposed to do? I tried to reassure myself I could fix everything once Gianna was back in Denver. Her dad was supposedly going to sell his house in Houston, pull out of his partnership with a group of other plastic surgeons and buy a home in the suburbs for him, Gianna and Chance to move into.

Chris had threatened Julie with taking her to court to get all her parental rights revoked if she fought him for custody. He probably wouldn't go that far, but Julie wasn't chancing it. Gianna wanted to live with her dad and Chris told Julie there was no way a judge would make her stay with an "unstable mother." Despite the vast difference in their ages, a judge also wouldn't want to separate a brother and sister. I imagined Julie was cooperating because she didn't want anyone to call her crazy on record.

Once Chris moved here, everything would get better.

My dad wasn't pissed at me at all about beating up Josh, but my mom was upset. She said while she understood why I'd done it she just wished none of it had ever happened.

We all felt that way.

She was also upset about my date with juvie court. My parents planned to be there to support me and hoped the judge would be lenient once my lawyer explained the situation.

A few times in the past couple weeks I'd wondered how Ian had fared. I was sure his dad eventually showed up to get him out of juvie. He probably had a court date scheduled, too.

Gianna must have not told Cece and her other friends about what had happened. When I saw Dante yesterday, he didn't mention anything about it. Since Dante dated Cece and Cece had a big mouth, I figured if she knew, he would also. Since Gianna didn't seem to want them to know, I wasn't about to tell anyone.

They all seemed to think she was just visiting her dad in Houston.

*****

Six days later, on a Wednesday, I found myself sitting with my parents outside the courtroom dressed in a suit, waiting for my case to be called. My mom was checking her lipstick again, a nervous habit, so I tried to soothe her, "It'll be fine, mom."

She forced a smile. "I know. I just always hate this part."

My smile came easily. Gianna was coming home next Tuesday and things were looking up. "Oh really, I thought you hated most the part where you see your baby boy in handcuffs."

"Remind me to take away your car," my dad grumbled on the other side of me.

"Look who it is, my good friend, Caleb," I heard from a few feet away.

I glanced up and barely stifled the instinctual groan. "Oh crap, it's the devil."

Ian laughed, motioning to my lawyer sitting a couple chairs down from my dad. "Is that your pit bull?" Before I could answer, Ian used his thumb to point to the guy in an expensive suit standing next to him. "This is my pit bull. He's here to get me out of trouble again."

"Where are your parents?" my mom asked him, recognizing Ian from my past run-ins with him over the years.

Ian had a blank look on his face. "What are parents?"

My mom was visibly embarrassed, unsure what to say.

Ian let her off the hook. "My dad is banging his new girlfriend in Cabo. He couldn't make it."

My mom gasped and I heard my dad do a choke-laugh combination.

She managed to get out an inadequate, "*Oh.*"

"What are you doing here, loser?" I asked Ian, wanting him to stop shocking my mom with his dirty mouth.

As his lawyer moved to converse with mine, Ian purposely took a seat on the other side of my mom. I leaned forward as he said, "My lawyer says the judge decided to combine our hearings since we committed the crime together. I'm not worried. My lawyer is really good. You should be grateful he's offering his wisdom to yours."

A middle-aged woman opened the door to the courtroom and called out, "Ian Crenshaw, Caleb Morrison." She held the door open while Ian, myself and our entourage filed into the courtroom. The room was small and since our crimes weren't exactly newsworthy, the pews were empty.

The similarities between court and church always amused me. My mom got on a Jesus-kick for back when I was in the seventh grade. She'd claimed the spirituality of it had helped inspire her artwork. In response, I'd suggested that many artists found alcohol inspiring. I'd been more than happy to get drunk with her instead of going to church. She'd made me recite a prayer. I'd been overjoyed when she'd moved on to meditation soon after that.

At church, I'd had to dress up, pray for my eternal soul and listen to an old dude in a robe lecture me. There were pews and an altar.

Court paralleled the church experience.

At court, I also had to dress up, pray for mercy and get bitched at by an old dude in a robe. They even brought the bible into both situations. There wasn't an altar, but the judge did sit up on his bench all high-and-mighty. He just didn't jabber on about the lord almighty. Instead of hearing about what a great guy Jesus was, I got to hear about what a piece of crap I was.

What Would Jesus Do?

Well, I was positive he would have kicked Josh's ass too.

After going through all the formalities the justice system required, the judge went on to explain why we were being tried together. Duh, we'd beat up the same dude. Then for each of us, the judge listed all the times we'd broken the law in the past.

Big shocker, Ian was even worse than me. What a criminal he was. I might have been caught with drugs, but the guy had gotten caught selling them before. Why would he need to do that? His dad was a millionaire.

When the judge mentioned we both had former assault convictions on our records, we glanced at each other in a weird sort of understanding. Reading from old court documents, the judge summarized the circumstances of our past assault convictions and I realized there was a difference between mine and Ian's.

I'd put a guy in the hospital because he'd hit a female friend of mine. Ian had done it for shits and giggles. Ian had been messing with some guy's girlfriend and when the guy got in his face about it, Ian went crazy on him.

A list of minor offenses was read through for both of us. Vandalism, petty theft, truancy, etcetera. What I took from the judge's lecture was that I'd gotten caught way too many times in the past four years.

It was strange listening to all of it, because that wasn't who I was anymore. I couldn't imagine pulling the dumbass stunts I had in the past now that I had Gianna in my life. Anything that took me away from her was a bad idea. I needed to be the kind of guy she deserved and could count on.

She was coming back in just six days. After getting court over with, I looked forward to a fresh start with her. I'd plan how to bring her back to herself and heal her hurts.

Last week, I'd done something completely out of character and checked out library books on psychology and helping victims of violence. I'd paid special attention to information pertaining to victims of sexual assault.

As much as it turned my stomach to think about what Gianna went through, I needed the advice on how to help her work through it. The books told me what kind of behavior to expect from her. Her emotions could include guilt, shame, embarrassment, depression, anger and detachment. Basically every crappy feeling possible.

I'd also learned all sorts of tips and methods for healing. I'd leave the hardcore therapy to whatever psychiatrist her dad set her up with, but there were simple things I could do to help her. When she came back, I'd gently start helping her heal.

"Caleb Morrison." As the judge stated my full name, I realized it was judgment time. "Ian Crenshaw," the judge also said. I glanced over at Ian to see his lawyer place a hand on his shoulder for support. We'd both entered a no contest plea as our lawyers had advised.

The judge continued, "Unfortunately, the victim was not able to attend the hearing. However, after reviewing the case, hearing the arguments from your lawyers, I've come to a decision." The sour expression on his face began to worry me. "I can understand the reason behind the brutality you both displayed. But as a judge, I have to follow the letter of the law. This wasn't the first instance of assault for either of you boys. Repeatedly, you've ignored the dictates of the law and done as you've seen fit. Had this been a first offense, probation would have been my course of action."

He sighed as if it was his life in the balance. "Seeing an escalation in the seriousness of your crimes, I feel it is in your best interests that I order a harsher punishment for both of you. A punishment which will hopefully deter you from future infractions that would see you in prison as adults later on in life."

I felt real apprehension start to build within me. Looking over at Ian, I took in his clenched fists. Suddenly feeling hot, I wiped the sweat off my brow and glanced behind me at my parents. My mom was already crying.

Turning back to the judge, I imagined him as the grim reaper in his black robe. "I order your parents to take you to the State of Colorado Youth Corrections facility in Pueblo by Monday morning at 9am. You will each remain at that facility in the custody of the state for the duration of 304 days from now, approximately ten months."

Hitting his gavel, the judge effectively ruined my life.

"True love stories never have endings."
-Richard Bach

**Book Three of the Beware of Bad Boy series
COMING SOON**

Also by April Brookshire:

**YOUNG LOVE MURDER
DEAD CHAOS
BEWARE OF BAD BOY**

For information on upcoming books, playlists,
my blog and newsletter,
Connect with me online at:

www.aprilbrookshire.net

Printed in Great Britain
by Amazon